BROUGHTUPSY

CATAPULT

NEW YORK

BROUGHT TUPSY

CHRISTINA COOKE

A NOVEL

Broughtupsy

This is a work of fiction. All of the characters, organizations, and events portrayed in this novel are either products of the author's imagination or are used fictitiously.

First Catapult edition: 2024

ISBN: 978-1-64622-188-2

Library of Congress Control Number: 2023936792

Jacket design by Sarah Brody
Jacket photograph © iStock
Book design by Laura Berry

Catapult
New York, NY
books.catapult.co

Printed in the United States of America

10 9 8 7 6 5 4 3 2 1

*For my family—in whose arms I found
safe passage across rough seas.*

from what we were
how imprisoned we are in their ghosts

—DIONNE BRAND, *Inventory*

BROUGHTUPSY

1996

MONDAY

SARA AND I WALK THROUGH THE HOSPITAL DOORS, up and around the large staircase as I recite the nurse's directions in my head. Take the hallway on the left, then another on the right, straight through the waiting room to a row of patient rooms, then turn, first door on the right— there he'll be. And there he is. My brother's hospital room smells like air-conditioning and antiseptic and the musty stench of something decayed. I glance up at the far corner, afraid I'll see a muted TV showing black smoke gathering above green trees like I saw the last time I was in a hospital, when I was nine and my mother was declared dead.

"Hey," my baby brother Bryson says, smiling up at me from his bed. He's already been here a week.

"Hi," I whisper.

He coughs—heavy, threatening, on the brink of something nasty. My girlfriend Sara hands him a tissue while my father watches from the hallway.

"Here y'are," Sara says.

Bryson's face spreads into a wide grin. Y'are, y-are, long drawl rolling easy in a familiar caress. He was two when we moved to Texas, only six when we left for Canada. He knows he's Jamaican. He knows what it says on his birth certificate, but there's something about slow-smoked brisket and fruit paletas and screaming *Hook 'em!* from football bleachers that makes him feel like he's where he belongs.

"How y'all doin'?" he says then coughs again, his small body convulsing.

"Akúa," my father calls from the doorway, gesturing for me to join him in the hallway.

But I don't move. I can't stop staring at my brother, watching the slow blink of his eyes and the way he squirms under the stiff sheets, IV lines pulsing red in and out of his sallow skin. He shouldn't be here. He's only twelve years old.

"We'll be right back, champ," Sara says, ushering me out of the room.

Out in the hallway, the doctor extends his hand to me, his head cocked at just the right angle to exude concern. "I'm sorry about all this," he says.

I stare at the gray hairs on his knuckles, my own hands limp at my sides. Daddy shakes the doctor's hand as Sara heads down the hall to give us space.

"Now that we're all here," the doctor says, looking from my father to me. "Bryson's sickness, it's hereditary. Passed down from parent to child just like eye shape and skin color."

Daddy looks at his knees.

"Is there a history of sickle cell in your family?" the doctor says. "Any extreme anemias? Blood-borne illnesses?"

I watch my brother through the small window as he coughs, his body retching with our mother's disease. Daddy buries his head in his hands.

"My assistant will be with you shortly," the doctor says. "She'll explain all the information we need to help you through this difficult time."

Sara looks at me longingly from the other end of the hall. She heard enough. She knows. I stay where I am, heavy as lead.

TUESDAY

I FLIP THE QUARTER BETWEEN MY FOREFINGER
and thumb, forefinger and thumb, as I stare at the gray
pay phone hanging on its hook. Behind me, I hear machines beeping and nurses shuffling in and out of patient rooms.
I have to do it. I have to call. Sliding the coin into the machine, I
dial my older sister's number.

"I know," my sister Tamika says as she picks up. "Daddy
called me this morning."

"When does your flight get in?" I rest my forehead against
the booth's cool wall.

She says nothing, her breath coming quick like she's struggling for air.

"Tamika?"

"Daddy didn't tell you?" she says.

"Tell me what?" I squeeze the phone. "Are you sick too?" I go
dizzy for a moment, knees threatening to give.

"No!" she says. "Praise be, I'm fine."

I exhale, relieved. "Then what?"

She goes quiet again, scratching sounds filling the receiver like she's fiddling with the cord. "I'm not coming," she says. "I can't come."

"What?" I wrap the phone cord around my wrist. A nurse rushes past me, a clipboard under his arm. "I'm sorry, what?" I say again.

Tamika stays silent as the nurse knocks on a door then lets himself in.

"He's sick, Tamika," I exclaim. "Yuh hearin' me? He's *sick*."

"I know," she says. "Can I talk to him?"

"Why can't you come?"

She goes quiet again, static filling the phone *pop pop pop* then clearing.

"Tamika?"

Nothing.

"Tamika, yuh cyaa be serious."

The phone line remains silent. She has nothing more to say. I unwrap the phone cord then stare at the crisscrosses of pulsing red on my skin.

"Are you serious right now?" I yell.

She sighs. "Why are you always like this?"

I don't know why, but I laugh. Our brother's in the hospital and she isn't coming, so I laugh and laugh and then I hang the phone up. I pick up the receiver, dial tone beeping, and I hang up again, and again, laughter rolling up my throat like fizz from a shaken soda. And I hang up again, and again, smashing the receiver against the metal clip harder, and again, and again, until Sara wrenches the phone out of my hand then pulls me away.

"Shhhh," she says as she wraps her arms around me, but I will not cry, I will not be soothed.

"Akúa!" she hisses as I push her away and march down the hall to my brother's room.

Slamming the door behind me, I pull a chair over to Bryson's bed. He looks up. I am here. He smiles. I am where I should be. I will not leave. I will not be known to my brother only as a voice through the phone. Running my hands over my braids, I force my face into a smile. I want to grab his lunch tray. I want to watch it smash against the far wall. Our sister isn't coming. "Eat your Jell-O," I mumble, pushing the tray closer to him.

"The food here sucks," he says. "Don't they have any enchiladas? Or taquitos?" He curls his hand into an O, then stares at the empty space between fingers and palm.

I know what he's thinking: scrambled eggs and melted cheese seeping through toasted tortilla, fresh and steaming as it wafts around the school courtyard.

"You remember Dave?" he says, wiggling his fingers as they bunch and grasp at nothing at all. "This one time," Bryson says, "me and Dave, we bought too many taquitos at recess. Daddy had just given me my allowance, so we bought too many and I saved some for lunch." He closes his hand into a fist. "Cold taquitos are gross."

"Should've made Dave pay for them." I sit on the edge of his bed. "Then they would've been his problem."

"But that's mean," Bryson says.

"But you would've had hot and free taquitos."

He chuckles as he picks up the plastic cup from his lunch tray, watching the green square jiggle in his hand.

"Eat," I urge him.

He slips a chunk in his mouth, chewing slowly then swallowing.

"See?" I squeeze his knee. "Not so bad."

He makes a face, pretending to puke, as Daddy comes into the room.

"Tamika should be here soon," Daddy says.

"She's coming?" I exclaim.

Daddy looks at Bryson and says to his son, "Her flight's been delayed, but don't worry, she'll be here."

Bryson puts his Jell-O down with a soft smile. He hasn't seen our sister since we first got to Texas, when he was two.

I grab my father's arm. "Is she really coming?"

"What are you going to say to your big sister," he says to Bryson, "when she arrives?"

Bryson thinks for a moment, fiddling with his gown. "I'm going to say, 'Sister, if you were in a burning car, who would you call: Batman or Superman?'"

Daddy laughs. I dig my nails into the cotton of his sleeve. Is she really coming?

"Such a smart bwoy mi have," Daddy says.

Bryson tries to laugh but his laugh turns into a cough. Closing his eyes, he sinks deeper into his pillow. He's breathing harder than before, air gurgling slow through his open mouth. I let my father's arm go.

"She'll be so glad to see you," I mumble to Bryson.

Daddy looks at me. "Yes," he says. "She will."

"Will she cook with us?" Bryson says, trying to sit up. "Does she like to eat?" Bryson loves to eat. He marks his days in meals, memories cataloged by the sensations on his tongue.

"Of course she loves to eat," I exclaim, leaning over Bryson and giving him a big big smile. "As soon as we get home, we're gonna whip up nuff cheeseburga and enchiladas."

"Enchiladas!" Bryson exclaims as Daddy chuckles. "And brisket! And rice and peas! And curry chicken but without the potatoes. I hate potatoes."

"Lawd, bwoy," Daddy says, pulling the blanket down over his toes, "yuh goi' eat yuhself sick."

Bryson smiles, closing his eyes. "I think I need a nap," he says, having worn himself out from saying so much.

"You do that, little chef." I lean over and kiss his forehead, his skin sweaty yet cold. Daddy fixes his pillow as I tuck the sheets under his hips.

Bryson touches my arm. "You'll be here when I wake up?"

I smile at him. "I'll fight anyone who tries to make me leave."

The doctor knocks lightly on the door. "A word?" he says.

Daddy and I follow him out of the room. From her seat down the hall, Sara throws me a small smile then a wave. Blinking fast, I look away.

"It's a long shot," the doctor says, rubbing his chin and handing over the forms, "but we're running out of options. The illness is progressing quickly. It's worth taking a look."

Daddy nods, signing the forms then handing them to me.

He doesn't read them—doesn't need to read them. He's been signing forms and sending Bryson and me for tests in hospitals since I was ten. The tests should've caught this. I flip through the pages and pages of fine print, trying to take it all in.

"Just sign," Daddy says, sounding tired.

Through the shut door I can hear Bryson coughing, fever getting worse.

"Are you all of Bryson's next of kin?" the doctor says. "If there are other family members, it'd be ideal if we could test them too."

I can't come, Tamika had said. She could and she should but she won't. Because why?

Because ten years ago, my father packed up my family and flew us over the sea. My sister and brother and me, Daddy flew us first to Texas before finally making home here, in Vancouver. I was ten when we first left. Bryson was two and Tamika was sixteen. In my head, Tamika's still sixteen.

Soon after we moved, Tamika left us abroad and went back home. All I know is that years passed with her in Kingston and us in Texas then Canada and Daddy calling her on the phone yelling—back then, he was always yelling—calling her wah eediat chile for leaving. "What about Mummy?" Tamika would sometimes say. "Who is here to tend to her?" Every time the line would fall into hard silence, just heavy sighs echoing until someone hung up. Our mother is dead so Tamika stayed behind, shaking her head in a never-ending no.

But now our brother is dying. And there's me, wanting my big sister. *What a eediat chile.* Signing the form, I press the pen against the paper so hard that it starts to rip. Our sister is in Kingston, delayed by a plane that will never land.

I watch my brother through the small room window, his breathing shallow as he tosses in his sleep. I hope he's dreaming of his sister sprinting through the airport, of her waving down the plane with her voice rising and arms flailing as she throws her handbag, her suitcase, throws her whole body, doing whatever it takes to stop the plane so she can climb on and come to him.

"Great," the doctor says, watching me sign. "My assistant will walk you to the lab to get the blood work started. Who knows, one of you might be carrying just the thing we need."

A nurse enters Bryson's room, introducing herself with a curt smile as she replaces one of the pouches hanging over his bed. Inserting the new needle into his IV line, she squeezes the pouch to start the flow—*dripdrip* Bryson's blood goes, *dripdrip* like counting seconds, losing time.

WEDNESDAY

WATER RUSHES THROUGH THE TAP, HOT AND unrelenting. Stepping into the shower at my father's house, I reach for the body wash next to shampoo next to two types of conditioner next to olive oil hair treatment next to face wash next to Bryson's body wash in a bottle shaped liked lightning. Before, in Jamaica, I only knew castile soap. You need face wash? Shampoo? Grab the castile soap.

I wonder about her in moments like these. I wonder what Mummy would think of this house, of Daddy directing trucks of gray dirt to silos caked in soot. Would she be relieved, happy to see us with trimmed nails and moisturized skin as we walk down roads where the asphalt never burns? Or would she be annoyed, wrapping her belt around her fist to discipline us for indulging in excess? I wish I could stop myself from wondering. My brother is in the hospital and my mother is dead. The exhaust fan whirs on, sucking the room cold.

"Call me if anything changes?" Sara says. "Good or bad?"

Stepping into the bedroom, I tie my robe around my waist. Sara's missed three days of class. This is my emergency, not hers. If she misses any more, she might fail.

I look at her cowlicked hair and milk-smooth face, her three brown moles beneath thin pink lips. She twirls one of my braids around her thumb then leans in close, the soft point of her nose pressing against the broad swell of mine. We are in love. We are twenty years old.

Sara stuffs her socks and toothbrush into her small backpack. She's leaving the suitcase we came with from our apartment for me. "Everything will be okay."

I glare at her. "Will it?"

She flinches then rolls her pants into a tight log, tucking them into the small crevice between her books on anatomy and biochem. She tells me she wants to stay, how she feels so awful, but it's all right if she leaves because my brother will be just fine. She smiles, cheery and bright. He'll pull through and I'll be back in class in no time.

I watch her as she shoves her sticky notes next to her deodorant and bag of dirty laundry and I can see it, she won't say it, the truth hiding behind the whites of her eyes. She's thinking about her test next week. She's thinking about keeping her grades up to flip her med school admission from conditional to guaranteed. Med school means going back to foil-wrapped taquitos and dark beers in cool bottles named after her great state. It means cicadas buzzing in fields of swaying hay and long dips in cool rivers feeding into the Rio Grande in her beloved Texas. I don't want that home. I say the word that's been lingering like sour meat on my tongue.

"No what?" Sara says.

"No."

"No, you won't call?" she says.

Standing back, I take her all in. "Take the suitcase," I tell her. "It's yours anyway."

FRIDAY

THE LAB RESULTS COME BACK. MY FATHER AND I, we don't have what Bryson needs. We watch through the window as a nurse wipes his brow.

"I'm sorry," the doctor says. He's looking right at us this time. He's being sincere. "This is one of those things we can't predict—what may trigger the anemia, how deep it may go."

A bag expands, contracts, making Bryson breathe. A small machine registers his heartbeat, black monitor showing a white line rising and falling in sharp peaks.

"He showed signs of improvement," the doctor says, "then his blood pressure dropped overnight and internal organs began to fail. He was clotting faster than we realized."

My brother's lying unconscious, thin and shriveled like a rind of old fruit. The nurse puts the rag away then reaches around him, slow and careful, and turns him over. My brother does not blink. He does not scream in protest against this stranger's touch. Expand. Contract. The machine beeps.

"Do we have your consent to take him off life support?" the doctor says.

"Jesus," I exhale. I was talking to Bryson just yesterday, and now we're taking him off life support?

The doctor looks at me. "Don't worry," he says, "your brother won't feel a thing. Brain activity slowed to dormant around five this morning."

"I wish you hadn't told me that," I mumble. I want to think of him as my Bryson, my brother, asleep but still here.

"Sorry," the doctor whispers.

Daddy flips through the pages on the clipboard, his hands starting to shake. He's done this before, tucked my mother away safe beneath red Kingston dirt. I watch him uncap the pen as he stands next to me in the hospital, doing it again. *Flip flip*, he barely breathes as he finds where he needs to sign.

"If you'd like," the doctor says, glancing at me, "if this is too painful, we can retrieve you once—"

"No," Daddy says, signing the form. "We're staying right where we are."

The doctor takes the clipboard. "I'm very sorry for your loss."

A nurse follows him into Bryson's room as I rest my forehead against the small window. The tube running from Bryson's mouth gurgles, sucking his spit through the clear coil then into a port in the wall. My brother cannot speak. He cannot swallow.

Hey Bryson, I murmur to my brother in my head. I watch the doctor silence the alarm on a beeping machine. Hey baby brother, remember your first day at school here in Canada? I close my eyes. Remember how upset you were?

"I just don't get it," you'd said. You were standing in the hall in our new house, still wearing your backpack. You were crying. "This one girl, she kept asking me, 'Do people in Texas ride horses to school?'" you said. "I told her no, we drive cars, *duh*. But she kept asking, 'Do you ride horses? Do you have to scoop poop every time you reach a stop sign?' And I said no, but everyone kept laughing. I didn't laugh. I didn't think it was funny."

I bent down until my head was level with yours. "You should've said yes," I told you. "You rode a horse to school and John Wayne was your gym teacher."

"What?" you said.

"Why not?" I shrugged. "If they want to ask stupid questions, give them stupid answers."

You wiped your damp cheeks. "Yeah," you said. "Yeah, okay. Yeah! Like, um, we use tumbleweed for floss."

I grinned. "And we turn cow poop into electricity for our houses."

"And, and," you said, thinking hard, "we make sushi out of snake meat!"

I laughed. "Every evening, we hunt wild cougars with our bare hands."

"Rawr!" you growled, crouching down on all fours as I spewed lie after lie to make my brother grin.

Now you're not laughing. I'm not sure if you're even still here. In the hospital room, the doctor signs something then moves to the end of the bed, sliding a thick tube between my brother's hips. Bryson doesn't speak, can't scream as the doctor tapes the tube to his knee then attaches the other end to a large clear pouch. The doctor pushes on his stomach, brown gunk seeping into the pouch as both nurses move to the head of the bed and start pressing buttons, turning things off.

"Daddy?" I murmur, my breath fogging the glass.

He lifts my head off the window, resting it on his shoulder as he wraps his arms around my waist. With a slight groan, he tries to lift me up like he used to, when I was a kid in Jamaica. Following his movements, I stand on my tiptoes just to make him feel like he can still do it, that nothing's changed.

Beepbeep the monitor goes, line climbing slowly. *Beep beep* the machine sings, line already beginning to fall, *beep* then I wait, I want to hear it but there's no more. Daddy buries his head in my shirt collar then lets out a long wail.

Our mother and brother, who art in heaven, hallowed be their names.

A Week Later

SATURDAY MORNING

"**H**EY. IT'S ME." I SWITCH THE RECEIVER TO MY other hand. "It's—hold on." I crane my neck to glimpse the clock above the departures screen. "It's five forty a.m., Vancouver time." I pause, listening to the stillness of my sister's voice mail. "I'm about to board my flight. So, um, guess I'll see you soon, sis." I sigh, no one there to meet my sound. "See you soon," I repeat, hanging up.

I called my sister after we left the hospital. I told her he was dead. Static crackled through the phone, puncturing the long silence, then she started to pray. So I smashed the phone against the wall so hard that the black plastic split at the seam. No, I didn't. I let her say her hushed words then at the end, just before "amen," I told her, "I'm coming home." "*What?*" Tamika hissed.

The little light clicks off as the flight attendant's voice fills the airplane cabin: "The captain has now turned off the *Fasten Seat Belt* sign . . ." I stare out the window, at the crisp white dents in sunlit clouds. I took out a line of credit for this. Breathing deep, I hug my backpack against my chest. I went to the bank and said I needed a student line of credit, showing them the schedule of classes I didn't intend to take, then bought a one-way ticket on a flash sale. Daddy offered to help pay. He had already sold the drapes, the couch, the living room table. "Is jus' me one," he'd said when I asked why. The hallway mirror, the reclining chair—all sold to whoever was the first to show up at our door and take it all away. "Why?" I asked him. "Are you moving again?" He kissed his teeth. "Wha mi need all dem someting fo'?" He gazed around the house, stricken and bare, then looked me over, a price tag materializing above my head. One plane ticket then gone, gone. I looked around at the house thinning like the gray hair on his head then told him no. "A line of credit is a loan," I said. "I'll *have* to come back to pay off a loan." He sighed, relieved. It's just him one.

So I bought the ticket. I boarded the plane that would take me over the sea and back to her. The last time I came close to seeing my sister was four years ago. Tamika and I, we usually talked on the phone—always on Sundays, always just before dinner—but that time she told me to go to the library and she would call me back via video call on the new machine she had just gotten at work.

"Video what?" I said. I'd heard of pagers and Sega, even about something called a PDA—but a video call? "Like, is it a call through the TV?"

Tamika laughed then said we'd fallen behind up there in the fancy first world.

The next morning, a Monday, I skipped my calc class and

made the trek across campus to my school library. I checked in then asked the librarian where the video call machines were. She pointed me to the computers outfitted with headphones and cameras in the back. Adjusting my headphones, I pulled the mic close. The image on-screen flickered, showing frothing rivers of static rolling across the small monitor.

"What the hell is this?" I whispered, waiting for the image to come into focus.

Sharp whistling filled my headphones, rising and falling in three crescendos of pleading sound.

I squinted at the screen. "Tamika?"

Pza-pza-pza the sound went as the static started to curve and take shape.

"Are you there?" I asked, pressing the microphone against my lips.

Pza-pza-pza, pause, *pza-a. Pza-u-a.* A-kú-a. She was saying my name.

"I'm here!" I exclaimed. "It's me! I'm here!"

Pza then I saw her, just barely, outline of her ears and chin as she leaned close to the camera. The static moved with her shape then stopped. Was she squinting like I was? Maybe she could see me too, shining through in distorted gray.

"Can you hear me?" I yelled. "Can you see me?" I pressed both hands against the screen.

She said something, her words coming in sharp crests of garbled sound. I pressed every button on the keyboard and turned all the knobs on the square monitor, trying to bring her into focus, to conjure her in flesh and blood and bow-legged bones.

Tamika's face appeared through the static, round and gray and there. My sister, dear sister. I felt my forearms tighten. I pressed harder, harder, then heard a soft *pop*.

The picture hiccupped then gave out as the machine died with a whirring *ahh*. Behind me, the librarian shifted in her chair. I slapped the side of the monitor as the librarian glanced at me then got up. Did I break it? The librarian's shoes kissed the carpet in muted *slap-slap*s. I pressed the power button again and again.

"Hey," the librarian said.

I smashed every button, but the machine stayed empty and spent. The librarian was almost to my seat. I think I broke it. Throwing the headphones on the floor, I grabbed my bag and I ran. I never went back to those machines again, avoiding that part of the library from then on out, afraid I'd break every single one of them with my hunger to bring my sister back to me.

The plane bounces twice, shaking me awake. Now, four years later, my brother is gone but my sister lives. So I'm not calling anymore. I'm going back. I'm going home. My seat belt digs into my hips as the cabin erupts in applause. We made it *clapclap* we're here *clapclap* well done, Captain—thank you, thank you, leftover custom from when they still called us the jewel of the British Crown.

"Ladies and gentlemen," the flight attendant says, "Air Jamaica is pleased to welcome you to Norman Manley International Airport."

Outside my window, mountains rise in rich green swells against gray sky.

"The local time is three forty p.m."

The grass, the mountains beyond—it's all so dazzling. Still waking up, I turn to the woman next to me.

"Are we here?" I ask.

She laughs. "Where else would we be?"

I keep searching as people around me start standing, overhead bins popping open. I'm here, in Kingston. I'm *home.*

"You're Jamaican?" the customs official says.

"Yes."

"What part?" he says, rifling through my passport with my birth certificate tucked inside.

"What part am I Jamaican?"

He looks up, adjusting a strap on his vest. "What part of Jamaica are you from?"

"Here," I respond. "Kingston."

It says so on my birth certificate, but he keeps watching me. He's grinning a little. We both know I don't need to include my birth certificate. It says in my passport that I was born here, that it is my birthright to pack up and come home whenever I please. But still, I wasn't sure—after all, it's been so long. So I shoved my birth certificate in with my passport then put the whole thing in his hand. I needed to know that I would be believed.

"Where do you live now?" he says.

"Canada." Like it says in my passport.

"Why?" he says, still staring. He isn't interested in reading it. He wants to hear me say it.

"Because that's where my father took our family."

"And your mother?"

I fidget with my backpack. "Dead."

"How?"

"Sickle cell." Like my brother.

"Where?"

"Here!" I exclaim. Exhaling hard, I smooth the front of my shirt to make myself calm. "Sorry. Here, in Kingston. Before we left ten years ago."

He keeps watching me as my lips move in propa English, my accent all dried up. "Yuh sure is Jamaica yuh come from?" he says with a chuckle, stamping my passport then signaling to the next person in line.

Walking toward baggage claim, I stuff my passport and birth certificate into my backpack. It doesn't matter how I sound. Behind me, I can hear the *stamp-and-swoosh, stamp-and-swoosh* of the customs official clearing the line. I know where I'm from. Huffing, I take three long strides then arrive at my carousel.

"Mek mi help yuh, missus," a porter says. He stands waiting in a black cap and maroon suit, his sparse beard speckled gray.

I force a smile. "No thanks, I'm okay."

"Yuh sure?" he says, smiling back.

"Yeah, I'm okay."

"Mek mi help yuh. Cheap! Cheapa dan all dem smaddy dem," he says with a wink.

I glance at the other porters leaning against the wall, trolleys parked in a jumbled mess. He reaches out to take my backpack.

"I'm fine," I say again, yanking it away.

"Miss—"

"No."

He laughs me off like I've made a silly mistake.

"Leave." Glaring at him, I set my face into a hard frown. "Go!"

The other porters take notice and chuckle. His smile cracking, he straightens up. He's taller than me, thinner, his arms too short for so much body. I look at his hands, callused and empty, and wonder if he's ever held a passport. I wonder if in all his years of carrying American bags, British bags, if he's ever packed up and carried his own. My suitcase arrives. He doesn't budge as I take it off the line.

"Move, please," I hiss, setting it on the floor then drawing up the handle.

He looks at the tag's white ribbon, YVR stamped on its tail. To him, I'm a foreigner. I am the protected lured here to spend and for him to serve. We both know what he has to say. "Yes, *miss*," he says, swooshing out of my way.

As I near the exit, all I hear are suitcases clacking and porters laughing as he crosses the room, pretending he can't hear them. And even though I shouldn't—I was born here, so I know I shouldn't—I'm laughing too.

Stepping into the muted daylight beyond the sliding doors, I cough then clutch my chest. The sudden change from air-conditioning to humid wind makes me wheeze. Coughing still, I walk to the curb, the crumbling concrete giving way to potholed road. Next to me is a woman in a teal church dress yelling at a man tying suitcases to a car roof with pieces of twine. Across the street is a patty stand with a long long line, and next to it are men in mesh shirts leaning against a wire fence, blowing smoke through their noses as they puff and puff, and there are children selling Pepsi and coconut water from beat-up coolers and porters pushing too-full trolleys behind white families, their skin garish against all the black, and next to me a child with black arms and black hair and down the sidewalk black and behind me black and I look and look as I pull my suitcase closer, sneezing against car exhaust billowing and patties baking and peanuts roasting in a pit hitched to a bike parked behind Corollas packed with eight, ten passengers and tour buses boasting AC destined for resorts behind policemen wielding batons in wide arcs of *move along, move along* as so many people, black, black, the sight of us filling me till drowning. My God, I'm home. And that's it, I'm gone, drowning beneath memories of my childhood rippling high in hot crests.

Chirp of tree frogs floating sonorous, each piercing chirrup rising on the wane of the last. I'm in my childhood home. I am nine years old. Eyes shut, I pressed my hands against the slick pane of my bedroom window to feel the cool damp night. Right here—the banana trees, the orange trees, the pumpkin patch that just wouldn't bear. Over there—the neighbor's house, the football field, the hill leading down to Spanish Town rising up in a smooth green curve. A dog barked; a door opened; a car engine sputtered, then stopped. Up here—the clothesline, the water pump, the pipe to the underground well that sometimes doubled as a slide. Behind there—the rosebushes, the old satellite dish, the gaping pit from that house that caught fire, the earth dark and red like a crusted wound. Fingers spread, eyes open—a lizard crawled across the glass, its white belly swelling red, then nothing, nothing, thick black nothing. A car started and sirens wailed and the frogs kept chirping, chirping. Is Anancy mek it. That's what Miss Lou said, the woman on TV with the big big smile and long brown dress and red plaid scarf tied around her head like a crown. It was my mother's favorite show. We used to watch it together, just her and me, every Sunday after church. Anancy trick poor Bredda Toad to jump ina wah pot o' bwilin' wata and eva since, *woi!*—long high whine curving up, ending shrill, like a scream. And the trees and the earth and the pigs' snouts and the reason why cows go "moo"—is Anancy mek it, so she seh.

"First time here?" the taxi driver says, bringing me back to present-day Kingston. Blinking fast, I take my hand off the car window. The taxi turns right as I watch the smoke from the patty shop trailing after us as we leave Arrivals. "No." I sigh. "It's just been a while."

"How long?" he says.

"Too long," I respond, leaving it at that.

My sister told me she'd meet me by baggage claim. I stood on the sidewalk outside the airport for almost an hour, watching the exit doors slide open then snap shut then open again, rain clouds reflecting off the clear glass. She never came.

I could've left. I could've gotten back on a plane, said *never mind* then hid my birth certificate in a place only I would know.

"How long?" the driver says again, turning toward downtown. Before I can respond, he pulls over to pick up more passengers. Four ladies pile in next to me, crocus bags on their laps. I open my mouth to suggest someone move up front but a man's already taken that seat, groceries crowding the space around his feet.

I'd forgotten this is how it works. You need to get somewhere? Great. So does everyone else, so small up yuhself! All dat space fi you one? Lawd Jesus, is joke yuh a mek. Small up yuhself an' mek room. There could be six, eight, sometimes twelve people in one taxi, cotching on armrests and even squeezing into the trunk, whatever it takes to get everyone to fit.

The women strike up a conversation about their haul from the market as the air-conditioning rattles, struggling to keep up. Afternoon heat seeps in, settling on us heavy and oppressive like a bad dream. I remember this feeling. I used to hate going downtown because of this feeling. Hugging my backpack against my chest, I try to distract myself, gazing at the storefronts and highrises giving way to two-story houses with gated front yards.

"Whitfield," the driver says, looking at me in the rearview mirror then pointing to the houses all around.

I smile at him, as thanks. The woman next to me reaches into her bag, her elbow digging into my ribs, and takes out a white cardboard box of cook food: jerk chicken, rice and peas, and a likkle bit of steam cabbage served by vendors with mobile grills on the side of the road. She offers some to the woman on her left as I smile, proud of myself. *Cook food*; I still remember what it's called.

"Duhaney," the driver says to me, careening around corners as the houses become smaller, closer together.

"Eh eh," one of the women says, "mi neva know is JUTA bus me jump in. Come in like tour guide."

The driver looks at me then says something to them, his patois too heavy for my ears. The women laugh, slapping the back of his headrest. The one in the middle leans forward and says something that makes them laugh harder, her patois thick like layers of lichen. I turn to them, wanting to share in their joke, their words flying hot and quick. They keep laughing as I keep staring, trying to translate their tongues rolling over vowels and slicing through consonants—but I don't get it, can't hear it, feeling like I'm listening through water. Biting my lip, I turn back to the window.

The driver looks at me in the rearview mirror then says something to them, easing onto the gas as the light turns green. Noticing my blank stare, he exhales slow, giving himself a minute to let his voice adjust.

"I'm dropping you off next," he says.

"Okay," I respond, then clamp my lips in regret.

The woman with her elbow in my side watches me from the corner of her eye, the conversation lowering to a hush. I've outed myself, my voice betraying a foreign lilt. *Am I Jamaican?* I wrap my hand around my neck.

Ten minutes later, we pull up to a low-rise complex that's three concrete towers poking up through the Kingston smog.

"Is you dis," the taxi driver says.

Hopping out of the car, I pop the trunk then hand him his cash.

"Where have you been?" Tamika says as I haul my suitcase onto the black gravel. "Didn't your plane land a while ago?" She rests her hands on her hips, her head cocked to one side as the taxi drives off.

My sister. She was supposed to pick me up. I should be upset but all I can think is, *My God, my sister.* Her hair falls in fat twists to shoulder-length, silver hoops dangling from her earlobes scarred with keloided skin. She's wearing a pink dress bunched up to one side—but her face, though, that same face: bushy brows angled high over my same cheeks, nose broad and royal above thick lips. She smiles, her lower lids bunching beneath brown eyes like Bryson's, like mine. She's lost weight.

"You've lost weight," I tell her.

"No," she says. "I've just grown up and stretched out."

It's been ten years. Squaring up to her, I realize we're the same height now. My neck tingles with memories of a childhood spent always looking up. "Is this the part where we do the tearful reunion?"

She chuckles, pulling me in for a hug. "Still trying to be the funny one."

"Hi," I murmur, smiling into her neck.

"Hi," she says, squeezing me tight. Giving me a proud pat, she pulls up the handle of my bag. "What took you so long?" She's walking toward the parking lot.

"You were supposed to pick me up. And, uh—" I glance back at the three towers. "Where are you going?"

"I haven't gone grocery shopping yet," she says. "What does Her Highness eat?"

"Can I at least put my bag inside first?"

"So you can get comfortable and whine 'bout how you nuh want fi leave? Yuh tek mi fi eediat?" She looks at the ground, my hair, a nearby tree, then finally at me. She shifts her weight from her left foot to her right. She's nervous. I'm fiddling with my backpack. I'm nervous too. Sighing, I let her lead me to a silver Corolla parked facing a cinder block wall.

"I'm still mad at you for not picking me up," I tell her, shoving her shoulder.

She forces a smile, then mumbles a quiet "Sorry."

She starts the car as I climb in, laying my backpack across my lap. *Click click* our seat belts go, filling the tense silence. She asks me about my flight. It was fine. I ask her about her day. It was fine. She taps her nails against the steering wheel, driving us out of the parking lot, as I rub my palms over the gray suede of my bag. Turning the AC to full blast, she swerves through rush-hour traffic.

I lift my left knee, then my right, feeling my sweaty skin slide all over the pleather seat. My body tenses, temperature rising as I keep glancing at her, thinking, *There she is.* The AC's blasting and it's starting to rain as I try to force my shoulders down but I'm just so tense. I can't stop looking at her, expecting her face to disappear behind a wall of shifting static.

People pass us on the sidewalk as we wait behind cars backed up at a slow light. They're hot too, the pedestrians, some of them holding plastic bags and backpacks as shields against the driving rain. The drivers around us wipe condensation from the insides of their windshields then use the same yellow rag to cool their shining brows. Our skin and the sky, they're all weeping, puddles forming in the dips above collarbones and potholes in the road and I remember now, I remember how much I hate this city. Kingston can feel so deadening in the afternoon, heat sitting stagnant as though taunting a hurricane to blow it free. I crack a window to catch wah breeze, smelling instead rotting trash and fruit sitting in stalls I can't see. I hate this city, but the scent of sweetsop ripening in downtown heat still makes my stomach moan.

Beep! Beep! a horn goes, two taps in quick succession implying, *Move nuh man!*

Beepbeepbeep! another goes, saying, *'Xcuse, missus, move up a likkle an' mek mi pass?*

Beeeeeeeep! saying, *Woi! Yuh try fi kill me? Tek time round dat cawna, sah. Mi dehya.*

Beep beep with every honk of the *beeeep* Tamika too *beepbeep* announcing, *I'm here.*

I'm here, so don't hit me. *I'm here,* so let me through. *I'm here,* so move up and make space.

We, all of us, we wait at stoplights and crosswalks, windshield wipers squealing in the hot rain. We hop over sodden grass and clogged drains, school khakis creeping muddy from the hemlines up. We run and we yell and we *beep beep,* announcing ourselves to the hills and gullies and thickening heat. I take a deep breath.

"Tamika," I murmur, unzipping my bag.

She doesn't hear me. She's too busy honking at a delivery truck that cut her off. Winding down her window, she yells something at the driver, her patois deep as the sea.

Opening my backpack, I take out the box and hold it flush on my lap. "Tamika, look."

"Look at what?" she says, indicating left but stuck at a red light.

I rub my hand over the dark wood. "Here he is, Tamika." I put the box on her knee. "Here's Bryson. I brought our brother home."

She looks down at the box then screams. Her body convulses as she jams on the gas, foot leadened like she's losing all her blood through her feet. All of it, all her color—gone. You ever seen that? You ever seen a black woman turn *white as a ghost*?

"Stop it," Tamika hisses, panting with her forehead on the steering wheel.

I laugh harder. We're facing a concrete barricade. Tamika managed to stop before plowing right through. Why am I laughing?

"Mi seh stop!" she says.

Cars behind us start honking, a few people leaning out their windows to yell something nasty as they pass. Leaning over, I wind Tamika's window up.

"You look like a ghost, you know that?" I settle back into my seat. "A black-white ghost."

She lifts her head off the steering wheel.

"I got tested, you know," she says. "When he was in the hospital. I went to Bellevue and let them draw my blood."

A bus rides its horn as it swerves around us. Tamika winds down her window and yells something then waves him on.

"You got tested?" I ask her.

"Yes."

"And?"

She shakes her head. She didn't have what our brother needed either. Sighing, I lean back in my seat.

"Why didn't you come?" I ask her.

She kisses the lacquered grain of Bryson's urn in a gentle *hello*.

"His funeral," I say a little louder. "The hospital, all of it. Why didn't you come?"

She throws the car into reverse, backing away from the barricade and back into traffic.

"Daddy would've paid for your ticket," I tell her.

Pursing her lips, she's as quiet now as she was when we first left, when Daddy made all his plans for our first departure. He said we needed a new start, that it was what our mother wanted. Tamika asked him if he'd crawled into her grave and asked her himself.

"*I* would've paid for your ticket."

She laughs. "How?"

I would've gone to the bank sooner. I would've gotten a loan just for her. But I don't bother explaining. She still wouldn't have come. After our mother died and Daddy came home with our U.S. visas, Tamika barricaded herself in her bedroom. She was going to start sixth form right there, at home, like her and Mummy had planned.

"Why?" Daddy yelled, threatening to break down the door.

She wouldn't answer. All she did was slide her scholarship

letter under her door, day after day, the seal on the top waxy and bright. Hampton School for Girls. Our mother went to Hampton, so she was going too and that was that. After a while, my father gave up banging and emptied the house around her, trying to smoke her out with silence. Tamika sucked the smoke in and turned it back on us all. For ten years, all I knew of my sister was her voice through the phone. I thought our brother dying would be enough to bridge this distance I didn't understand.

"Why didn't you come?" I ask again. Still silence—so I ask again, and again, till she turns on the radio and switches to the news.

"Why didn't *you* come?" she murmurs. "All dis time since yuh leave yuh fadda house an' yuh neva come look fo' me?" She grips the steering wheel tighter then grimaces.

I stare at her, head spinning as I open and shut my mouth like a gutted fish as we continue down the road with the press and pause of traffic.

We are sisters, not friends. Our shared blood means there is nothing here to earn, to covet, to lose. We will remain sisters no matter what happens, no matter what we do or don't say or how many years we're apart. I want to scream in her face but instead I clamp my lips against all my angry questions. You wanted me come to you? But *you* left *us*. And for what? I chew the inside of my cheek. Tamika keeps driving, sighing with the relief of knowing I'm due no answers. My sister did not come to my brother's funeral. That's that.

"Which supermarket are we going to?" I huff.

Tamika says nothing, just indicates to turn right.

SATURDAY AFTERNOON

AS MY SISTER AND I DRIVE ALONG TOWARD the supermarket, I keep watching the people out on the streets, wanting to lose myself in the slap of slippers against asphalt and creak of pushcarts on wet road. But my tongue's bloated, gagging me with the weight of things I'll never know. Why didn't you come to the hospital? Why didn't you come for your brother? *Why didn't you ever come back for me?*

Tamika was sixteen years old when we moved to Texas. I don't remember how my father got her to come. All I remember is her stone-faced and mute in the airport, on the plane, and through customs until the rental car in Texas. She was pudgy then—denim overalls pulled taught over the soft pooch of her stomach, her hair jet-black and wild. Bryson was two, just two, his first molars starting to poke through. Closing my eyes against the Kingston heat, I slump into my seat, emptying myself, and I am ten again. I am in the back of the gray minivan in Texas with my brother and sister, my nose against the window as I stared at the huge signs lining either side of the asphalt road.

The signs, there were so many of them, big, then bigger, competing in bright colors. Square and towering: COME IN TODAY FOR AN OIL CHANGE AND FREE TIRE ROTATION. Another, squat and plain: FORD, BUILT TEXAS TOUGH. Long, blue, flapping against the side of a brick building: BEST BUY COMING SOON.

Smiling, I leaned forward then whispered to Tamika, "What if you went into Best Buy, but what you got was not the best buy?"

"Shut up," she said. "You're not the funny one." *Clickclick* her seat belt went as she craned forward toward our father, wedging her palm between the strap and her skin.

"I funny!" Bryson squealed.

"No, you're the annoying one," I muttered, slumping deeper into my seat.

"Daddy?" Tamika said. "Where are we?"

Hunched forward, Daddy squinted at the street signs, comparing the names on their green metal to what was scribbled on the paper in his hand.

"Daddy?" Tamika said again, her voice just louder than a sigh.

"Lawd, man, stop yuh noise!" he said, gripping the wheel so tight that his brown knuckles gleamed white.

Tamika recoiled, letting the seat belt sink into her neck. Smooth bass riddim floated about the van, tom-toms joining on the swell. Reggae. Just like home, Daddy had said.

The minivan swerved to the right then stopped. Rain pattered against the roof, filling the cabin with a rolling hush. Daddy got out, *ding ding ding* of the driver's door ajar. I slid open the side door as Tamika unclipped Bryson from his seat.

Stepping onto the stone walkway, I gazed up at the single-level house painted faint yellow with white double doors facing a thin strip of lawn. Daddy fished a key from the mailbox then let himself inside.

Blinking, hands shielding against the rain, I looked over at a cluster of palm trees huddled by a gate leading to the backyard. Brown and dying, the palms drooped over the gate's spikes like washing hung out to dry. They looked like they'd never borne coconuts, stalks peeling and fronds all dried up. I walked over and pressed my hand against the soft bark.

Eyes closed, there—the water pump, the guava tree, the banana trees so rough and tall. Breathe in to smell the hot Kingston air. Instead, I smelled car exhaust, muddy creek bed, and the humid stench of Texas trash. Rainwater dripped off my thumb in slow-moving disappointment.

Ova de hills an' across Jah valley, we go deh already. The sound of the radio blaring brings me back to Kingston, to Tamika's car and the heat settling heavy as my sister drives on. *Call His Majesty, we*— Tamika changes the station. The sounds of synth piano pump through the speakers followed by the skank of the lead guitar.

"Do you remember our house in Texas?" I murmur.

A young boy knocks on my window as we stop at a red light, holding up bags of june plum for sale. Tamika shoos him away.

"No," she says. "Why would I? I was only there a week."

We pass a police station, a barbershop, vendors selling box lunch and freshly roasted peanuts on the side of the road. I watch my sister's face in profile. Bryson and I lived in that house for four years. He learned how to be a Cub Scout in that house. That's where he learned how to scramble eggs, his favorite, how to make them soft and fluffy with a sprinkling of sharp cheddar on top. In that house, he learned long division, about the rhythms of the moon and stars, and about the importance of signing his own name. Sighing, I look away. She was only there a week.

The music picks up. *Dere were nights when de wind was so . . .* We pass clothing stores and apartment buildings, steel security bars showing through their long windows. *Dere were days when de sun was so . . .* the singer croons, her voice melding with the riddim. Tamika pulls into a gas station. I put my hand on her arm as she flies the catch for the tank. *All de tears turn to dust, and mi jus'—* Tamika turns the engine off.

"Look at me," I say to my sister.

"Akúa, Jesus." She exhales in frustration. Turning back the key, she revives the radio to drown me out. The piano spins off in a solo, the singer cutting in on the reverb. *I finish cryin' in de instant dat yuh lef'.* I squeeze her arm, our skin growing hot in the idle car.

"What?" she spits. "What is it? What do you want?"

The drums pick up as the piano staccatos underneath.

"Are we actually listening to a wannabe Celine Dion right now?"

She pauses.

"This is really happening?" I exclaim. "We're listening to the Jamaicanized Celine? Celine with too much jerk seasoning?"

Her lips twitch in a begrudging smile. A saxophone screeches in, harmonizing with the vocals—*But when yuh touch me like dis*. I'd forgotten this happens here. If there's a hit song by a crooner, a song that's meant to break your heart, a Jamaican singer will perform a cover set to a reggae rhythm and the Kingston radio stations will play that cover so often that the only thing you'll soon want to break are the speakers themselves. An attendant in a yellow polo knocks on Tamika's window. Still chuckling, she asks him to fill the tank up.

"Does Celine know this is happening?"

"I don't know, Your Highness," she says. "Let me go ahead and just call her up."

An' yuh hol' me like dat as we sit and wait for the pump to click off. Tamika hums along, sometimes mouthing the words beneath her breath. This is a bad joke, but still, even then, the car settles into a gentle easiness with the swing of the steel drums. Tamika sighs, hooking one hand through the crook of the steering wheel as she rests the other on top of the gearshift. She looks steady. She looks open.

"Why did you leave us?" I murmur.

Tamika stiffens, turning the radio up as loud as it will go. The attendant returns with her change. She counts the coins then drops them in her purse, never looking at me. Punching the button, I watch the dial fade to black.

"Why?" I say again.

"Why are you here?" she says, staring straight ahead. "Why now?"

"Because our brother—"

She laughs. "Stop it," she says. "Stop lying in our brother's name. Why did you come?" Signaling right, she pulls onto the thoroughfare then revives the radio. The station's moved on to a new song but I can't hear it, I don't know what it is, air turned stale and strange. Why am I here? *Why did you stay?* Tamika isn't going to answer. She's leaving me. She's gone. I stare at my hands, trying to settle.

I remember when Tamika first left me. It was nighttime at the new house in Texas. We had been there three days. It was almost time for her to go, to return home.

As my father unpacked box after box in the kitchen, I slunk away into a bedroom, bumping against sealed boxes with *Tamika's Rm* scribbled across their sides. When we were getting ready to leave Kingston, she had packed up her boxes and stacked them to one side to take with her to Hampton. Daddy made her put the boxes on the truck, saying Texas was going to be her home too.

There were only two boxes open, one full of clothes and the other showing cassettes and posters and a white bottle of rattling something lying on top. I pulled out the bottle. Cod liver oil pills. The bathroom tap shut off. Snapping forward to face the door, I hid the bottle behind my back. The bathroom door creaked open, followed by Tamika's feet thudding toward the kitchen. Exhaling, I sat down.

Cod liver oil, little pods of golden goo. Popping the bottle open, I shook a few out. *Take two*, Daddy had said. It was after breakfast, a Sunday, dark smears of corned beef drying on my plate. *Take two*, he'd said. *No*, I'd said. I remember Mummy chuckling, sipping her tea as Daddy stood over me. *Take two*, he'd said, *or else you can't have any watermelon*. I loved watermelon.

"You can keep them," Tamika said as she pushed past.

I stood up quick, pills spilling onto the floor.

Tamika glanced at the pills. "Leave them," she said. "Always hated them anyway."

I smiled up at her. "Remember that time—"

"Wait, you've been in my stuff." She turned around, glaring at me. "I told you not to touch my stuff." I slumped against the wall. She hopped onto her bed then pulled out a folder, *Sixth Form Orientation* printed on its front.

Remember that time when I wouldn't take my pill, so Daddy reached across the table and forced me to take it? *It's good for you*, he had said, *it'll build strong bones*. But I wouldn't do it. I wouldn't take it. So he'd put the pill against my lips and pushed and pushed till the coating gave way and that goo, that nasty goo filled my mouth and made me gag. I brushed my teeth eight times, but my breath still smelled like rotting fish. Ha ha ha. Wasn't that funny? Ha ha ha.

I didn't say any of this out loud.

"You know you're not going back, right?" Tamika said, her eyes on the folder in her lap. "I am, but you're not."

"What?"

"You're never going back," she said then turned the page.

"Where?" I asked.

"Home."

I looked around the room, at the naked walls and unpacked boxes. "What?"

"This isn't home," she said.

"Then—" Boxes and boxes. "Then—"

She got up. "This isn't home," she announced, "not for me." She walked out, weaving through boxes of her things never to be unpacked.

"Where are we?" I looked around at her magazines, her pictures, her cloth poster with the wooden rod that always banged against the window back ho— Then, then where were we? I stumbled into the hallway, hearing plates scraping against shelves in the kitchen and the crush of cardboard boxes being broken down.

Her clothes, her shoes, her netball we once used to knock down that bird nest back ho— The bottle slipped from my fingers, smacking against the carpet. I kept looking around, boxes and boxes, then—soft splat underfoot. Oh no. Feel the oily slime beneath bare toes. They were supposed to be good for me.

"Akúa?" Tamika called.

Pills, everywhere. Step, *pop*. Sharp release of rolled-up rot. Good for me. *Pop, pop.*

"Pickni, yuh hearin' me?" she said.

Why didn't they give Mummy better medicine? Why didn't Daddy fix this so Mummy wouldn't have to go away? I covered my ears against question after question piling up in a big mess. Why did we have to leave? Why is Tamika the only one who gets to go home? I smashed them, I smashed them all. Good for me.

Holding a handful of goo, I smeared it against her netball, her folder, her pile of clean new shirts.

"Are you touching my stuff?" Tamika shrieked.

Stench of rotten fish, dank and nauseating. Smear it everywhere—on her cassettes, her walkman, across the front of her magazines.

"Akúa?" Feet advancing.

Pop pop pop, smash them all.

"Akúa!"

My sister stood in the doorway, fists clenched and eyes wide. "What did you do?"

I thrust out my hand. Smell it. Smell it! Smell the stinking, rotting fish. Just like home.

Tamika turns left, pulling into the supermarket parking lot here at home. The music on the Kingston radio switches, a Diana Ross song this time sung to the beat of a slow ska tempo. Tamika's asking me what food I like to eat so she knows what to buy. Her lips curl and brow twitches and I want to leave her, I want to fling open the car door and run and run.

I undo my seat belt. "I'll eat whatever you feed me."

She grabs her purse and leads the way inside.

SUNDAY

21 Days Left

"**H**OW MUCH FARTHER?" I ASK. WE'RE BACK IN the car, swerving through Kingston traffic. Tamika usually goes to church on Sundays but instead she's taking me somewhere else. She won't say where.

"Impatient like wha," Tamika says with a chuckle.

We continue up, up, passing half-built houses with rebars turning red with rust. Silence fills the car like smoke as Tamika turns down a side street, pulling off the road then parking on a green bank. I turn to her, my questions shattered into splinters burrowing deep into my insides.

"Wait, so, we're here?" I ask her.

She chuckles. "Excellent deduction, Your Highness." She slides the lockjaw into the grooves of the steering wheel then hops out of the car.

Across the street are a series of houses, green roof then red roof then red, the first two with flowers and the third without.

"Where are we?" I yell, climbing out of the car.

"Lawd 'ave mercy," Tamika says, "how could you forget? This is our old neighborhood. I figured since, y'know," she gestures to my bag with my brother inside, "that maybe you'd want to see."

She walks ahead, umbrella spread against the light rain. I used to fantasize about coming back, about busting down the door then lying on the living room rug until the new family left and my own family came home and we would roll around and make all the rooms smell like us again. But now, standing on the side of the road, all I see are plain houses with clogged gutters and a stray dog strolling in between.

Tamika walks up the driveway of a one-story with faded red shingles above cream-colored walls, front gate lying to one side in a mangled mess. She climbs the steps as I stand by the swing set, watching the wooden seat rock back and forth, back and forth. Tamika rounds the corner to the backyard. I don't remember much about this house. I remember the living room and kitchen, but I couldn't tell you if Tamika's room was bigger or smaller than mine. I watch the swing and my skin starts to tingle, wooden seat rocking like aged wicker creaking, and this I remember, how could I forget? I remember the hospital chair groaning as I pushed my legs and rocked back and forth, back and forth. I was nine years old. I couldn't stop pushing, making the chair creak harder, louder. I came to this swing after and kept on rocking. My mother was dead.

The humid smell of soggy dirt and the dull whir of hummingbirds hovering seeped in from beyond my mother's hospital room window, mixing with the *beepbeepbeep* of machines out in the hall. I watched the hummingbirds flitting here, there, tiny little things, wings beating so fast I couldn't even see them, just looked like hovering curls of beak and tail.

The TV in the corner droned on with the man on screen staring, dark brown eyes beneath drooping folds of light skin. *Seaga*, the scrolling text read, *Prime Minister Edward Seaga*. Bryson yawned, squirming in his stroller. Daddy looked at me as though about to say something soothing, then looked away. Back and forth, back and forth, she's—no.

"Political maneuvering," the man on TV said, pronouncing every word with a sharp smack of his lips. He's speaking the Queen's English, proper English, the kind spoken by people whose fridges never empty and lights never go dark. "These demonstrations are nothing more than political maneuvering meant to upset . . ." The screen switched to images of streets barricaded and empty, of black smoke swirling above Constant Spring Road. The nurse came in.

"Shut it off," Daddy said.

Mummy, she, she seemed fine, just sick like always, then something started beeping—loud, whiny, one long screech. So they came in and took her, said not to worry, that they'd fix her like always. Then, then they came back, said she— The stripes of Daddy's shirt blurred with the brown of Bryson's head as I rocked the chair harder, faster, back and forth, back and forth. Now Tamika was standing in the spot where Mummy's bed used to be, her body shaking like breathing set to staccato.

—she's dead, they said. What? She's dead. No. Back and

forth, back and forth. She's dead—no. She's—no. Back forth back forth nonono.

"We will not be bullied!" Seaga said. "We will not back down!"

"Shut dat dyam ting off nuh man!" Daddy yelled.

Tamika doubled over, balling her hands against her chest. The nurse crossed the room to the TV then switched the sound to mute.

"We," Daddy said, "we have to go."

The nurse looked at him. Behind her, the TV changed to burning trash barrels turned roadblocks as crowds paraded past, their faces gnarled and angry. She walked over to Daddy and put her hand on his shoulder.

"I'm sorry," she said.

Daddy stared at the floor and rubbed his hands against his thighs. "We have to go!" he said again.

The nurse dropped her hand then stood aside, freeing the path to the door. From beyond the window, I could hear sirens wailing.

At home I lay in front of the television holding the plastic hospital bag of my mother's things—her comb, her earrings, her silver necklace with Jesus in crucifixion, his face rubbed smooth from years of fervent prayer. I was not crying. Tamika was in her room, wailing so loud that her sobs echoed all the way to the kitchen, while Bryson slept in his crib. I couldn't figure out why I wasn't crying.

Daddy moved all around me, picking things up then putting them down like everything was alien, like he was seeing his house for the first time. He picked up my shoes, putting the left foot where the right should go and the right in place of the left. He picked up the coasters, turning them over one by one then arranging them in a lopsided circle on the settee. He picked up a piece of paper and started reading under his breath.

"What's that?" I asked.

"A will," he said.

I watched him as he kept reading. A will? In school, they taught us that a will was an action, a verb carried out by your body. Verbs are things you do and nouns are what you do them with, so I didn't know what he was holding. That was a sheet of paper, a thin piece of noun. Why wasn't I crying?

Daddy muttered under his breath as I kept watching him, waiting for him to reveal the truth of what was in his hand. After a while, I pulled my mother's shirt from the bag so I could inhale her smell and will myself to cry. Closing my eyes, I breathed in. Peppermint—not the kind from gum; the soothing kind, like what comes wafting from a fresh cup of morning tea. Daddy snatched the shirt out of my hand.

"Wha wrong wid yuh?" he yelled. "Dis look like napkin? How yuh so stupid? Like yuh no 'ave no broughtupsy?"

My body flinched but I stared at him all the the same. Pacing about the room with my mother's shirt in his fist, he screamed and screamed until his voice rivaled Tamika's and all I heard was noise.

Daddy bent over me again, yelling so loud that his voice turned hoarse. His eyes were tomato red. His nose was starting to run. There was noise down the hall and noise in my face so

Bryson woke up, blinking hard and starting to pout. I still don't know why, but I took Mummy's shirt then pressed the fabric to my father's face, smothering him with my mother's smell. Daddy breathed in quick gasps, quieting to a calm hush. Peppermint. He picked me up, his body caving, and held me tight. I let him carry me around the living room as he cried into my neck till my collar was soaked through. Over his shoulder, I could see the swing set swaying in the breeze.

"Hello?" Tamika snaps her fingers in front of my face. "You coming?" she says, leading the way toward the backyard. It is 1996. I am twenty years old.

I look down at my hands, moving my fingers one by one. Walking to a window, I press my nose against the glass to see who lives here now, who calls this place home.

"I don't think they're here," Tamika says.

"You know them?"

She nods. "They let me walk through once, before they pulled up the flowers and gutted the front rooms."

I walk around to the backyard, wondering if my bedroom is still a bedroom and what color they've painted the walls.

"That's where you fell when you were six." Tamika points to a large PVC pipe jutting from just below the back door and curving down into a concrete slab on the ground. "You used to use the pipe as a slide," she says, "which was fine. Saved Mummy and Daddy the trouble of expanding the swing set. Then one day you fell. I don't remember how, but you fell from the top then landed on your face and knocked out your two front teeth. No one would have cared, except they were your adult teeth. They had just finished coming in." She pokes at my gums as I swat her hand away. "Mummy put your teeth in milk while I washed out your mouth and Daddy called around for a dentist. It was a Sunday. Yuh know how hard it was to find a dentist on a Sunday?"

I stare at the spot where pipe meets ground, concrete giving way to weeds. I remember how upset Daddy was about my teeth and Mummy rubbing my back to keep me calm, but I don't remember the feeling of falling. All I remember is the pain.

"We should go," Tamika says. "We need to leave before the neighbors think we're here to break in."

This is a place that's supposed to mean something, this squat split-level with cracked tile stairs.

"Are they fun?" I ask Tamika.

"Hmm?"

"The people who live here now. Are they fun?"

She chuckles. "They're a family. This is their house. What does *fun* have to do with it?"

I glance at the roof. "I hope they're fun." This is a place that's supposed to be deeper than feeling, stronger than blood. I hope the new family painted the walls orange, or red, and turned the bathroom into a closet and my bedroom into a disco. I hope they have a young daughter, or a full-grown son. I hope they do backflips off that pipe that would put my sliding to shame.

"Come on," Tamika says, walking back to the front of the house.

"I'll meet you by the car."

She nods then continues on. Once she's around the corner,

I unzip my backpack then flip the latch on Bryson's box, opening it just wide enough to slip my hand inside. Running my
tongue along my teeth, I sprinkle a few pinches of my brother
on the broken concrete. Glancing at this house, I wonder if our
mother would've let Bryson have his own room, like Daddy did,
or would've made him share with me. Spitting into my palm, I
rub my hands together until his dust makes a soft paste.

"What're you doing?" Tamika says. I hadn't heard her come
back.

I hold up my hands.

"So you just," she pauses, "just *brought him with you?*"

Turning back to the house, I give her a small shrug. "I put
him in my bag. I put my bag on the plane. That's that."

She comes a little closer. I open the box like she might join.
She stops then turns around, standing guard around my privacy
to do this thing she doesn't understand.

I smear him onto the pipe, against the wall, into the grass
and dirt and remnants of my old blood. I hope the new family
laughs. I hope the new family fights, screaming till hoarse. I
hope they mistake these streaks for filth, hosing it off and washing him deep. And when they come skipping, ready to play, I
hope my brother grows into thick weeds that will break their
fall, bones intact.

"Don't get that on the seat," Tamika says, watching me climb
into the car.

"What?"

"You need a napkin?" she asks, unzipping her purse.

"Tamika," I look at my hands, "this isn't dirt."

She's bent over her bag, riffling between her compact, her lipstick, a small tub of petroleum jelly. I force my hand under her nose, bits of our brother lining the creases of my palm. She jerks her head away.

I look at her narrowed eyes and hard frown. I know this look. I've seen it on my father and imagined it on my mother. This is the look that says, *No more*. This is look that says I should stop before I find myself in pain. But she's twitching, eyes darting side to side like she needs to pee. I've never seen this in my father. I think she might be scared.

"Tamika," I murmur, sliding my hand over her forehead and nose as Bryson sticks to her skin like an Ash Wednesday kiss.

"Don't," she says, holding my wrist. "Please don't." She looks like she might weep.

I pull my hands back and put them in my lap as she starts the car.

"Let's get our nails done!" she says, forcing her face into a too-broad smile. She pulls back onto the road, tapping her thumbs on the steering wheel as she stares straight ahead. Tamika, it's me.

"What's your favorite nail color?" she says. "I always get green. I feel like dark colors keep dem shine fi longa." She clicks on the radio, scrolling past a dancehall station then a Spanish station then back to dancehall then on to the evening news.

It's just me, Tamika. I touch her arm. She moves away. Me, your baby sister. She drives faster, knuckles bared to keep from losing control. Watching her, I consider asking again, *Why didn't you come?* She might speed up and drive us over that hard edge. Guts smeared against red earth, I might finally know her truth. She takes the corner so fast that the tires start to squeal.

"Red? Black? What's your favorite?" she says, merging into traffic. Not merging—slicing. She slices across two lanes of traffic, front bumper scraping a car's taillight as she cuts off two taxis to put us in the outer lane.

Sighing, I decide to let her be. "Let's go to the beach." I force a smile. "Doesn't the beach sound fun?"

"You sound like a tourist," she says.

I wipe my hand on my jeans. "I never paint my nails. I don't like getting them done." I've only painted them once, after losing a bet to Sara. She couldn't stop laughing as I squirmed in the parlor chair—so, later, I pressed the hot pink of my nails against the insides of her thighs.

"Sara and I broke up."

Tamika overtakes a truck, turning up her wipers to fend off its spray.

"I miss her," I mumble. "I know it needed to end, but—"

"Am I supposed to feel sad for you?" Tamika says, her broad smile gone. "Yuh get put up inna wah big house a foreign an' tink yuh can change law like God." Tamika slams on the brakes, tires squealing behind a red light. "What you did with that girl was wrong," she says in the Queen's English, proper English, the language we were taught that is of righteousness and truth. "Filthy and strange and wrong."

Here it is. Here is how she'll make me hurt. Clenching my hands, I watch her eyes steady. As my body starts to tense, she lets her shoulders relax. She looks at me, chest heaving and triumphant. I am wrong and she is right, just as it should be. We are sisters, not friends. I bite my lip so hard it starts to bleed.

Traffic thickens as we turn onto Slipe Pen Road, horns starting up again in competing *I'm here*s. I loved Sara. She was my girl for four years, my friend for nine. Tamika parks behind a kei truck squeezed in a back alley. I glance at her, our same-colored eyes meeting in a hard stare.

"You're wrong," I growl.

Tamika kisses her teeth as she undoes her seat belt.

It wasn't strange. I *loved* Sara. "You're wrong!"

My sister sighs. "Do you know what they do to people like you here?" The soft pitter-patter of rainfall fills the small car. "Listen to me," she says. "No restaurant will serve you. No barman will let you drink."

I stare straight ahead, windshield turning wavy with crests of hot rain.

"They will laugh at you and spit in your face," Tamika says. "Are you listening? They will stone you. They will bring their machetes and guns. *Listen to me, mi seh!* They will butcher you in broad daylight then leave you to rot. And the police will pay you no mind."

Taking a deep breath, I crack my knuckles to make myself calm. It's okay. She doesn't know any better.

"Tam—"

She clamps her hand over my mouth to make me listen. "Akúa, Your Highness," she says. "You must denounce this life. Are you listening? You will know no peace."

A higgla hustles past, the wheels of his pushcart slipping on the muddy pavement. I want to yell, *No*, and *You're lying*, but there's barely enough space inside her hand for me to breathe. So I do the only thing a little sister can: sticking out my tongue, I lick her fingers and palm until her hand turns moist and she lets me go.

"Now you're diseased too." I smirk as she stares at her wet hand. "Isn't that how cooties work?"

"You stupid child," she hisses, and then she slaps me across the face.

I stare at her, stunned.

She slaps me again. I put up my arms in defense. She punches me in the stomach, in the head, punching me again and again until my ears start to ring.

"Yuh tink is joke me a mek?" she screams, punching me on the arm, in my back. "That dem goi' treat yuh nice-nice 'cause yuh learn from book abroad?" She hits me again, and again, anywhere her fist can find soft flesh.

"I'm sorry!" I shriek.

She pauses, breathing hard. The kei truck in front of us starts its engine, black smoke billowing from its exhaust pipe. I touch my sore chin as the stench of burning oil seeps in around the closed windows.

Tamika pushes open her door, muttering under her breath as she marches up the alley. I watch the smooth swing of her steps as I sit in the car alone. I hate you, but I don't know where I am. Tasting blood, I open my door then swing my legs around. I hate you, but I don't know where else to go. I lag behind as she leads the way.

"Watch yuhself!" a woman yells.

"Sorry," I mumble.

"Easy, gyal!" another woman says, shoving me out of her way.

Rows of women line both sides of the street, hands moving fast as they finesse the hair of the people seated before them. A few have curlers, frayed plugs jutting from groaning generators. Some have nail polish, fake eyelashes, boxes of hair dyed indigo and orange with streaks of platinum blond. Overhead there are blue tarps draped between buildings in a makeshift ceiling, water seeping through small tears like pockmarks leaking rain.

"Where are we?"

"Mathews Lane," Tamika says.

"What is this?"

"What does it look like?" she says.

This is an outdoor salon. Stuffing my hands in my pockets, I follow her like a wayward child. I lick the welts on the inside of my cheeks and I feel beat down, I feel small. Tamika doesn't turn, just walks straight ahead. I wonder what my mother would think if she saw us fighting. Would she jump in and defend me or simply shake her head then look away? My ears are ringing and I don't know where else to go, so I hollow myself, curling in, and I am small again, I am following my sister down a hallway to the bathroom to get ready for school.

The collar of my school uniform flopped over and stuck to my neck, starch wilting in the early morning heat. It was the week after my mother's death. I reached for the tap out of habit, forgetting we were in a shortage. There hadn't been water in the pipes in days. Back forth back forth she's— I grabbed my backpack and ran down the hall.

"Listen to me, man," Daddy said, a diaper balled in his fist, "mi cyaa bodda wid yuh foolishness. Mek de delivery, den mi will pay yuh. Yuh tek mi fi fool?"

Daddy's pacing in front of the television, his body interrupting the clips of cars overturned and garbage burning, of men parading with signs and machetes over their heads. That man comes on, Seaga, his lips smacking on mute.

"What's happening?"

Tamika glanced down at me. "Daddy's ordering water."

"No." I pointed at the TV.

Tamika sighed. "They're demonstrating. The streets are blocked off. No school today."

On TV, policemen in thick suits and black helmets lined up on one end of the street, standing shoulder to shoulder like a human wall. I slipped my hand into Tamika's as we watched the streets across Kingston burn, bringing school and work to a halt. The mob on TV slammed their machetes down on the policemen's heads as children threw rocks and pieces of broken bottles. Some of them looked like they were the same age as me. Some of them looked like they might have been in my homeroom.

"Why are they demonstrating?"

"Because they want a better life," Tamika said.

"So," I looked up at her, "why don't they just go to school?"

Smirking, she tugged on my cornrows. "Great observation, Your Highness. Maybe we should make *you* prime minister."

"Don't call me that." Only Mummy could call me that. "Your Highness" was her special nickname for me, only me.

Daddy looked at us—"Lawd, man, wha kinda business you a run?" he yelled into the phone. He looked at us again, intent with something to say—"'Ole on nuh man," he said into the phone. "Mi seh 'ole on!" He looked right at us—"*Pumping surcharge? Wha kinda foolishness yuh a chat 'bout?*" Then he pointed out the window.

Tamika followed the line of his finger to the tops of green bushes smothered by clouds of burning diesel, to the neighbor's house all dark and locked up. They left three days ago, gone a foreign fi good.

"So?" Tamika said, fidgeting as she stared at the empty neighbors' house.

Daddy moved the receiver to his cheek. "Mi neva raise no eediat," he said. "We have to go."

"You?" Tamika hissed. "*You?* Raise *me?* Is Mummy, yuh mean."

Daddy gripped the receiver tight. I looked from Tamika to Daddy, my shoulders hunched in the tense quiet. Daddy raised his fist in one quick move so I ran to my brother, wanting to shield him, and pressed his face against my chest.

"Shhhh," Daddy cooed. He had pulled Tamika close, his arm around her waist and her head on his chest as he bounced up and down, his whole body moving to soothe her weight. "Is all right," he said. "Shhhhhhh."

"What about Mummy?" Tamika said with a sob.

"Is all right," Daddy said, still cooing, never answering.

A few days later, I was standing on the seat of our swing, my mother's shirt in my hand. Eyes closed, I bent my knees and pushed the swing back, and forth. Back, and forth. Over there—the football field, the orange trees, the red red dirt so hard and rich. Up there—green hills dotted with white houses, power lines stretching up in thin black lines. Right here—the clothesline, the rosebushes, the—Mummy's rosebushes, back, and forth—

Behind there—the bus terminal, the neighbors' house, the three-story mansion someone started to build then stopped. Back, and forth. Here—the banana trees, the neighbor's old satellite dish, the lime tree Tamika sometimes made me crawl under to get the ripe fruits nestled in the center. Back, and forth. She's dead. Back, and forth. I convulsed in a deep sob.

My mother is dead but that's all right, though, can't that be okay? Just as I had always known her, my mother would be off in another room and she would be surrounded by people I didn't know and she would miss me, I am her daughter and she would miss me, love booming silent like Miss Lou on mute. I imagined her lying in a green bed propped up against soft pillows and laughing, laughing, as she spread her arms to swallow up the whole room inside her quiet web. She was somewhere close I could not go, somewhere felt but absent, ever-present as the breeze. How could I have been so ungrateful? I had no reason to cry. A pair of strong arms lifted me off the swing and held me in the air.

"Akúa," Daddy said. "What are you doing, hmm?"

He cradled me in his arms. I looked up at him, my eyes burning like I was swimming in the salt sea. He had freckles around his eyes, dark and scattered like constellations. I wondered if Miss Lou would say Anancy made them too.

Why did we leave? Because my father saw the streets burning and stock market crashing and his wife was dead. His wife was dead. So he turned to his three children and said it was time to go.

Now, ten years later, I'm back home in Jamaica. I'm at Mathews Lane with my sister, looking around at the women painting nails and braiding hair in this outdoor salon. Tamika walks toward a woman with an empty seat.

"How yuh do?" the woman says.

"So so," Tamika responds, sitting on the piece of cardboard spread over the wet ground. They fall into an easy rhythm, chatting like everybody around them, the whole alley buzzing like a hive.

"Akúa," Tamika says, "you want beads on the ends of your braids?"

The hairdresser chuckles as I kiss my teeth. Beads in my hair like dem skinny white pickney dem at the northcoast resorts. Like a visitor, like a tourist. I hate you, but I came back for you. Licking the wound on the inside of my lip, I say nothing against this new hurt.

Tamika tips back her chin for the woman to shape her brows,

the blade gliding smooth over her taut skin. I imagine shoving Tamika's head so the blade nicks her, drawing a thin line down her cheek till she's bleeding like me. I hate you, so I need to go. Tasting blood, I gather myself up then sneak away into the crowd of roving black.

I look in on clothes shops and sidestep homeless men sleeping against the sides of locked-up buildings. I pass a furniture store with neon-yellow walls and a patty shop with fogged-gray windows and the burnt remains of a corner shop, blackened zinc jutting from hard rubble. I pass a supermarket with a plus sign on its sliding doors and billboards for security companies showing stocky men behind dark glasses standing next to burly German shepherds lunging with teeth bared. I keep walking, afraid someone will know I'm lost if I stop.

"'Ello, missus," someone calls. "Buy wah umbrella?" A man holds out two umbrellas from his table of things for sale.

"'Ay, pretty gyal," another man calls. "Smile fo' me nuh?" He pats his lap as I spit at the ground between his feet. Surprised, he jumps back as I hurry across the road and through the nearest door I can find. I collapse into the restaurant's booth farthest away from the door, the smell of oversalted potatoes clogging my senses like a quick-set cold.

"Oi!" a woman yells from behind the counter. "Yuh haffi awda!"

"Two-piece chicken meal," I tell her, rising to my feet then pulling out a five-hundred-dollar bill.

She gives me a wary look then hands me my change. Hunched in the booth with my food, I watch the rain streaking down the windows. No sister, no Sara—just me. Flies buzz around my head as I suck the meat off the bone in the empty cook shop.

I wish I could call Sara. Call her and say what? I stuff fried potatoes into my mouth. She was there from the beginning, the first person I met at my new Texas school. I had been in first form in Jamaica, but sixth grade was where the Americans put me *because of your age*, they said. I was ten. I was supposed to be with algebra and worm dissection and Shakespeare's sonnets but they put me back with factors and syntax trees and papier-mâché volcanos spewing dyed-red vinegar and baking soda. I met Sara during morning break on my first day. *Recess* was the name Americans had given it. Not *morning break* like in Jamaica, *recess*. Everyone hung about the cobblestone courtyard in chatty clusters, some lining up for juice boxes and foil-covered somethings for sale on a table nearby.

My skin tingled with pinpricks of early morning heat as I took a bite of my sandwich. I was eating my favorite food, Easter food, the only thing my father could find in the half-unpacked kitchen as we rushed out the front door. I was holding bun and cheese: dense brown bread shaped like a spider's back with a thick slice of Tastee cheese in the middle, salty yet creamy like a wily surprise.

"What's that?" someone said.

Peering up, I saw blue eyes and three moles beneath pink lips.

"I'm Sara," the girl said. "I like your name." She plopped down next to me, her skirt settling against mine. "What's that?" she said again, pointing at my sandwich. She leaned closer and started poking at my food. She wasn't going away.

"Nice to meet you, Sarah," I huffed.

"No." She grabbed my arm. "My name's Sara. *Saaaraaaa.*" She dropped her jaw to exaggerate the *a* like opening wide for the dentist.

"Well, nice to meet you, *Saaaraaaa.* My name's *Akúúúúú-aaaaaa.*"

"*Akúúúúaaaaaa,*" she said, the two of us sitting there with our mouths hanging open like little kids playing see-food.

Someone looked over at us then muttered, "What the hell?"

Sara burst out laughing. "I was named because of my eyes," she said. "So blue and fair like the sea, like Sara. My grandpa named me." She sat up straight, chest proud.

I smiled back. "Your grandpa sounds like a nice man."

She giggled then shoved my shoulder. "So what is that?" she said, pointing at my sandwich.

"Bun and cheese," I mumbled.

"What?" she said.

"Bun and cheese."

"Um." She smiled. "Say that one more time."

Bun and cheese. I didn't understand why she couldn't understand me. I groaned and tried to wave her away.

"No no." She grasped my arm. "I want to know."

She tek mi fi fool? I'd already said it three times. I turned my back to her, staring at my shoes and waiting for her to leave. She stayed right where she was, legs swinging as she waited. Sighing, I gave in and said it again, loud and slow. She watched my mouth and followed along, her lips miming mine.

"Oh," she said with a laugh. "Bun and cheese. I hear you

now." She looked down at my sandwich. "Is it some sort of hamburger?" She came a little closer. "Is that what hamburgers look like where you're from? And why is it so ugly?"

Ugly? I looked down at my delicious bun, so round and brown like Anancy's back. Sara went over to the snack table, then came back holding one of those foil-covered somethings. She ripped away the wrapping, smells of bacon and melted cheese swirling in the rising steam.

"Breakfast taquito," she said, noticing me staring. She took a bite then showed me the inside: scrambled eggs and melted cheese wrapped in something like roti—and bacon, that's what I remember most, salty smell of slow-cooked bacon.

"Ta-qui-to," I repeated under my breath.

"Never heard of it?" Sara said.

I shook my head.

She took another bite. "It's pretty tasty, not gonna lie."

Tasty how? I wondered. Was it soft? Salty then sweet? And what's that bread, that roti-looking bread? Holding my bun, I tapped her on the shoulder. She paused mid-chew. I pointed at my bun then her mouth, at her taquito then my stomach; a bite for a bite as a mouthful of hello. She swallowed, eyebrows raised.

"Uh," she stared at my bun, "you want me to eat *that?* That's, um," she stood up. "Thanks, but I'm just, I'm not," she patted her stomach as the bell started to ring.

She slipped away, disappearing into the shuffle of people rushing to class. I looked down at my bun as my stomach growled, loud and disappointed.

Now I'm staring at the bare chicken bones on my plate,

disappointed still. Swatting at the flies buzzing around the cook shop, I dump my trash in the bin and stack my tray on the small shelf. I open the door, humidity making me wheeze, then make my way through the hazy city.

For three hours I wander around downtown Kingston, popping in and out of stores and watching performers in the streets. When I start to get tired, I find a bazaar, then the bus depot, then I figure out which line will take me up Red Hills Road and back to Tamika's apartment.

"Where have you been?" Tamika yells as she yanks the apartment door open. "Are you trying to get yourself killed?"

I glance up at her, my key suspended midair.

"Where were you?" she says again. "Why won't you listen to me? Yuh tink is joke me a mek about how dem treat smaddy like you?"

I stay silent, letting her think the worst of me. Sealing my lips in a hard line, I let her reel and think the worst about herself. I am her baby sister and she lost me. What if I'd gotten myself killed? What if her only sister had turned up dead? She trails after me as I walk to the bathroom to strip my rain-soaked clothes.

"And you come mess up mi house wid yuh nasty—" she says, slipping in and out of British English as she points at my muddy shoes.

I take off my socks as she keeps yelling, her voice filling the small apartment. I unzip my jeans and pull my shirt over my head. She yells like our father. I'll be sure to let him know she's made him proud. She drops to a mumble as I unclip my bra and kick off my underwear, nipples clenching in the sudden cold. I watch her as she heaves, spent from her sermon.

"Nice nails," I murmur, then push the door shut.

MONDAY

20 Days Left

"**N**o," I respond, staying where I am.

"What?" Tamika says, her car keys in hand.

"No." I dig my thumb into my pajama pants. "I'm not coming." I can hear the blue cotton giving way with a soft *pop*.

"*What?*" she hisses, coming closer.

"I'm going out alone." I look out at the power lines looping between the short buildings. I hate you, so I won't follow you.

"If I were to put you outside right now," Tamika says, "you wouldn't know your ass different from your ear."

"Give me a map, then."

She laughs. "So yuh can go wonda de streets like a dyam tourist? Might as well save yuhself de trouble and give de gunman yuh purse now."

"I don't carry a purse," I murmur. Don't you remember? I hate the weight of bags on my shoulders or straps in my hands. I don't like purses. I carry a wallet. You should remember. I've been this way since I was young.

Tamika walks around the couch and throws my shoes on my lap. "You're not going out alone."

"Yes, I am."

She walks to the front door. "No, you're not."

I take a deep breath. "Tamika—"

"Come," she says. "Mi seh come! Come and see your mother." She opens the door and waits. My mother?

So now we're sitting in the car, engine off and facing the back of the car park. It's hot today, as usual. Tamika has her hands on her head and keys on her lap. We've been in the car for five minutes and I'm already starting to sweat. Tamika breathes deep, trying to keep herself in control.

"Can you crack a window?" I ask.

She doesn't move, just breathes in   and out, in   and out. Sweat begins to collect in the crease of my elbows.

"Can you crack a window *please*?"

"I should have known," Tamika mutters, turning the car on.

With the AC at full blast, I turn on the radio and start flipping through the stations. Tamika smashes the black button to turn the radio off as we merge into traffic.

"I should have known this is how you'd be," Tamika says, driving us out of the car park. "Do you know why Mummy came up with 'Your Highness'? Because you used to stomp and scream until you got your way."

A young boy knocks on my window as we stop at a red light, holding up bags of plantain chips and frozen bottles of water. Before I can decide, Tamika shoos him away.

"You'd scream like you just couldn't go on living unless

everything shifted to make space for you. Like when we were young," she says, "Mummy used to make eggnog every Christmas morning from scratch. The proper way, the Jamaican way, with brown sugar and fresh nutmeg and white overproof rum. You hated it. You'd hear the blender going on Christmas morning then scream for hot chocolate with little marshmallows sprinkled on top."

We slow behind a bus, its exhaust billowing across our windshield. Churches and shopping plazas line either side of the road with clumps of thick trees squeezed in between.

"So when you were four, or was it three? I don't know, when you were young enough to not yet piss me off," Tamika says, "Mummy gave you a small bowl of eggnog. No liquid, just the white foam off the top. 'Snow,' she told you, 'for Her Highness on Christmas morning.' I thought you'd scream your head off but you didn't. You stuck your face in it till the peaks stuck to your chin then you ran around the house yelling, 'Look! I'm Santa Claus!' Mummy just laughed. She was the only one who knew how to make you hers."

Tamika laughs as she dips in and out of lanes, trying to beat traffic.

"Every year after that, Mummy would make eggnog, and every year, she would give you your bowl of snow." Tamika glances at me. "Don't you remember?"

I chew on my lip. I'm supposed to say yes, but all I remember is her lying on the couch with me on the floor and Miss Lou on the TV. I remember *Ring Ding*, Miss Lou's show. "He is everyone and everything," Miss Lou would say. Everyone and everything, with her big big smile and gesturing hands like performing in a pantomime. And that laugh, that booming laugh that came rolling forth with every *ha ha ha*. After church, I'd crumple onto the floor in front of the television glued to the dancing pictures as Mummy lay on the couch behind me, nothing to give.

This is how I knew her: Slouched in a chair or flat on the couch, coughing and yellowed and smiling. She'd press play on Miss Lou then close her eyes, smiling, thinking—about what? I didn't know. So I'd lean against the couch and rest my head on her knee as Miss Lou stood with her arms spread wide and told how crab got his shell and where lizard got his croak and why night owl isn't called Pattoo. "Is Anancy mek it!" she would say, then laugh and gesture and laugh till the speakers crackled with static. Sometimes Mummy would reach for me, so I'd scoot a little closer until my cheek touched her palm. And every time, she'd soothe my skin in small circles then tell me to keep watching, that one day I'd understand. I was a bright girl, so I'd watch the show again, and again, and every time Miss Lou would laugh, and Mummy would laugh, and I'd sit there, watching them, left out of the sweet sweet joke.

Tamika swerves right-left-right to avoid a pothole. My sister and I are six, almost seven years apart. In my memory, my mother is yellowed and silent, eclipsed by Miss Lou on TV. I've never met her mother, loud and cunning as she whips white snow from eggs and rum. And Bryson . . . I open my mouth to explain but my lips close again, tucking in on themselves at this gulf of knowing that keeps us apart. Tamika switches gears, speeding up.

"Do you remember Bryson?" I ask her.

Somewhere behind us, I can hear sirens howling. She stops behind a taxi as traffic comes to a halt.

"What was his favorite color?" I ask her.

"What does that—"

"What was his favorite food?"

"What are you going on about?"

"He had two things on his face. What were they?"

She throws up her hands. "Lawd God, chile—"

"Don't harass me about Mummy when you abandoned us abroad."

Tamika pulls onto the shoulder, letting a police car pass. I squeeze the backpack between my knees, box inside. I don't know her mother and she'll never know my brother. Tamika exhales hard before merging back into the lane.

"Orange," I murmur. "Bryson's favorite color was orange. And he loved taquitos. And he had dimples on either side of his face. And why did you hit me?"

Tamika maneuvers through a roundabout then turns the radio on. The sounds goes fuzzy then comes back with a traffic report about the accident we just passed. Three cars. Minor injuries. Motorists advised to avoid. I stare at the black dial, all gutted and mixed up.

"At Mathews Lane. Why did you hit me?"

She sighs. "Because you need to learn."

We slow behind a bus, its brakes squealing as it slows down.

"Is there always traffic here?" I ask her. "Just seems like every time we leave the apartment, we come up against traffic." I'm babbling—but it's something, anything, to switch the subject to something safe. The bus speeds through the four-way stop as we inch forward then wait our turn.

"Well, this is a city," Tamika says. "Cities often have traffic." She glances at me. "They do have these abroad, right? Cities?"

I roll my eyes. "Har har, you're such a funny one."

We both laugh, a little too long and a little too loud for such a thin joke.

Tall billboards warning against speeding pepper the side of the road, the green and white metal offering shade to the higglas set up underneath. I see a higgla's table full of star fruit, chocho, otaheite apples, and big plastic bags of guinep.

"Pull over."

"You're hungry?" Tamika says.

"Just pull over."

She swerves onto the shoulder. A woman approaches, bags of fruit in each hand.

"Guinep!" I yell, winding my window down.

She holds out two bags, each filled with bunches of dark green globes on thin brown stems.

"Just one," I tell her.

Looking at my lips, the higgla smirks then pushes both into my hands.

"Just one!"

Tamika leans over me. "Jus' one, she seh!"

The higgla says something angry, her patois coming fast and hard. She heard the way I talk. She thinks I can pay more. Tamika fires back, the two of them arguing in words I can't understand. Tamika takes one of the bags and shoves it back into the higgla's hands.

"Thirty dollars," she says to me.

After paying, we pull back on the road as Tamika reaches onto the back seat. She puts a piece of newspaper on my lap.

"Because they—"

"They stain," I respond, nodding. "I remember." Tearing a hole in the bag, I pull two globes off the stalks then hold one between my teeth. The green shell cracks, giving way to pink fruit, fleshy and wet. The first time I saw Sara—really *saw* her—she was leaning over me, her breasts rising in freckled curves to pink nipples. "Like guinep," I told her, feeling that first ache to knead her skin with my mouth. The small bulb rolls across my tongue, sticky flesh dissolving around hard seed.

"Taste good, eee?" Tamika says, hearing me moan.

Turning right, we pull into a flat green park with red-dirt roads. MEADOWCREST MEMORIAL GARDENS the metal sign says. Counting under her breath, Tamika focuses on row after row of small stones. At the fifteenth row, she throws the car into park.

There's a man in the opposite field of the cemetery looking at me, his blue pants rolled up over bare feet. Tamika gets out, slamming the door behind her. The man has a rag in his hands and a bucket of murky water next to the gravestone by his feet. He nods. I nod. He bends down and starts to scrub. Opening the car door, I feel the shock of something electric, like the itch of a phantom limb.

"They're so close together," I whisper, looking down at gravestone after gravestone as I creep closer to my sister.

"We live on an island," Tamika says.

"I know." I hop over a gravestone. "But there's no space for people to pay their respects without stepping on somebody else."

"We live on an *island*," Tamika says again. "I don't think the dead will mind."

I think of all those corpses touching, bones against bones with dirt packed close. All dat space fi you one?

"Here," Tamika says, her voice dropping to a reverent hush. She kneels in front of a small gravestone laid flush against the ground. Crouching next to her, I trace my finger over the white marble engraved with cursive text. *Gone to Be An Angel*, the text reads above two hands clasped in prayer. *Mariela: Wife. Worker. Mother of Three.*

"There's no casket under here," Tamika says. "Just a box with her ashes. Daddy said he needed the money to pay for the new house abroad."

I put my arm around Tamika then look at the gravestone of my mother. I touch the earth above Mariela, this *Mother of Three*. My fingers digging into the dirt, I stare at the hands clasped in prayer and feel——

Soft splash of water hitting stone. The man's working in our part of the cemetery now, a fresh bucket of sudsy water in tow. I press my forehead against her stone and feel——

Splashscrubscrub, he hums a song under his breath, tapping the rag against the hard earth to the beat in his head.

"Dis one too, yuh hear?" Tamika calls.

He stands up. "Mek mi jus' do it now, missus."

Moving back, I kneel on the gravestone just behind. He

squats down, using the calluses on his hands to scrape off the thick dirt before polishing the marble with a small rag. He takes care to clean out the text, scooping the moss from the deep *W*'s and yellow streaks in the small *T*'s. He gives it all a rinse with a handful of water. Scraping away the last bit of grime, he stands to leave.

"Wait." I grab the car key from Tamika then rush down the row. Unlocking the passenger side door, I open my backpack and grab Bryson off the floor. Tamika looks at the box then at me, eyes wide as I come rushing back.

"Let's leave some of him here." I unlatch the box.

Tamika holds her breath as though she might accidentally inhale him.

"Come on." I grab her hand. "Come on, now."

Bryson moves through her fingers softer than sand. She exhales, closing her hand around a small handful. I grab some too then latch the box shut.

"Is what dat?" the man says.

"My brother."

"*Our* brother," Tamika says, sprinkling him in a thin circle around our mother's grave.

I follow suit, my hand trailing hers.

"From dust we are born," Tamika murmurs, "and to dust we shall return."

The man tips his bucket over our hands, washing Bryson down, down, mother and son mingling in the red earth. We watch the water as it puddles, recedes, no sound passing between us save the squeal of far-off car tires. The man picks up his bucket then turns to leave. Tamika hands him fifty dollars, for the water spent, as we follow him back to the road.

"Did you bring clothes for church?" she says.

I clench my lips shut. Not this fight. Not today. Slipping into the car, I wedge Bryson between my feet. Another traffic report comes on, says the highway's been cleared in all directions. Tamika looks over at me as though about to ask about church again—then she kisses her teeth, letting it go.

TUESDAY

19 Days Left

I'M SITTING ACROSS FROM TAMIKA, MY EYES still groggy and clothes carrying the sour smell of sleep. Every morning I wake up, waiting for the heat to become as commonplace as the tree frogs chirping melodiously through the night. And every morning I wake up annoyed, peeling away sweat-soaked sheets and wheezing through humid air.

Tamika's still in her robe, her headscarf balled in her lap. Between us are two bowls, two spoons, a box of Apple Jacks, and shelf-stable milk.

"Cereal?" I grab the Apple Jacks. "I'm finally home and all you're giving me to eat is cereal?"

Tamika snorts. "Sorry to disappoint, Your Highness, but believe it or not we Jamaicans are not untouched natives who walk around eating jerk chicken and yelling, *Irie!* all day." She snips the corner off the milk. "We eat cereal and toast just like everybody else."

Sighing, I look around the small kitchen. "I'd forgotten you're the sarcastic one."

She laughs. Her floors are white linoleum, her ceiling an ash-gray. There's a window next to us, small and square with red grilles slicing the bright morning light. There's a dinged-up toaster next to the gas range, oven door soot-black and creaking from years of heavy use. Her counters are two long stretches of bleached-clean Formica, a wooden bowl on the far end holding one degge degge piece of yellow yam. Her walls are an empty pale blue.

"Let us pray," Tamika says.

Sunlight glints off the gray hairs dipping in and out of her twists as she bows her head. In her living room, she has a coffee table, a radio, a small TV and VCR in front of the settee. On the far wall, she's hung her university degree from UWI framed by her Hampton graduation cords, blue and white thread fading from years in sunlight.

I remember when we were kids, Tamika used to take Mummy's Hampton cords and wrap them around her wrists. Most times our mother would say nothing, just left Tamika to play, but sometimes—these were the special times—Mummy would nod then hum Hampton's graduation song beneath her breath. Smiling, Tamika would drape the cords over her shoulders, her head held up high. She'd make me pretend to be the headmistress as she marched across the living room toward me, Mummy humming and laughing as she watched.

I turn my head and keep on looking around the small apartment, but that's it. There's nothing more to see. There are no pictures of me or Daddy or Bryson, no signs of to whom she belongs. In the ten years we spent apart, I imagined our faces smiling down on rooms cluttered with bright rugs and heavy furniture. I imagined a plush couch buried beneath too many pillows, and little knickknacks covering her bookcases and TV. In my mind there was music, always music, something loud and raucous as she did the Bogle dance from one room to the next. I imagined her comfortable. I imagined her surrounded by soft things. The bare floor squelches beneath my sweaty feet. She is as closed now as she was at sixteen, setting off for Hampton—all by herself.

"For food and friends and all God sends," I mumble.

Eyes closed, Tamika smiles. This is the same prayer our mother said before every meal.

"We praise Thy name, oh Lord," she finishes. "Amen."

Tamika digs into her cereal, smacking her lips to fill the kitchen with some sort of sound. I still remember Mummy's prayer, can say it faster than recalling my own name. I am Anglican. But I am not religious. I am proudly Anglican, as much Anglican as I am Jamaican, but I am not religious. That doesn't make any sense. In my first week, still adjusting to the new school in Texas, I had to choose: Be Anglican or be whatever the teachers wanted to call me. So I made a choice. I made myself known. We were in history class being put into groups of threes for a class project.

"Hey," Sara said as I sat down next to her. "This is Barrett." She pointed to a ginger-haired boy next to her.

He tossed his bangs off his eyes. "What's up?"

The teacher, Sister Marlene, was writing on the board. *Read the passage on pp. 18–20 then compose a short play about these events*, she scribbled. "All group members must have speaking parts," she announced. A few people groaned.

"Um," Sara said, touching my elbow, "sorry for, sorry about recess. I was just . . ." Recess. Taquito. My bun and cheese. She laughed, sinking lower in her seat. "I was full. Sorry." She chewed her bottom lip.

"Battle of San Jacinto," Barrett said as he read the passage through his bangs. "I wanna be Sam Houston."

I stared at the painting beneath the paragraphs in my book, at the brown and white people posed about on the swath of green. "What's the Battle of San Jacinto?"

Sara looked up.

"What is it?" I said.

"Battle of San Jacinto," she said.

"I heard him. But what *is* it?"

Sara fiddled with the corner of her book. She didn't understand what I was saying. Groaning, I skimmed the passage and tried to figure it out for myself. Everyone else was already picking roles and practicing as though they knew this battle like the back of their hands. I couldn't read fast enough, and we were being graded. I needed to know what to do. So I gave in. Turning to Sara, I cocked my head then scratched my scalp, feigning confusion like the buffoons on TV.

"Oh," she said. "Do you not know what that is? It's the battle for Texas's freedom—"

"Remember the Alamo!" Barrett yelled, his index finger and thumb pointed in the air. He made a sound, a *pop* then throaty push of air exhaled through rounded lips: *pu-kyiou, pu-kyiou.*

"Barrett!" Sister Marlene yelled. "Quiet down."

He lowered his hand as Sister Marlene kept pacing. Barrett waited till she turned then pointed at her back: *pu-kyiou.* "You know any Mexican?" Barrett said, looking at me.

"Spanish," Sara said. "The language is called Spanish."

Barrett shrugged. "Whatever. So do you?" he said, his gaze still on me.

"Yo quiero queso." I turned to Sara. "That's all I know."

Sara laughed. "I want cheese?"

I cracked a smile. "Yeah."

"Yo quiero queso," Barrett repeated under his breath. "Sounds cooler when you say it." He grabbed his pencil and started writing in his textbook. "So you're the Spanish guy—"

"Mexican guy," Sara said.

"What*ever.*" Barrett kept writing. In his book. He was writing in his book. All of them—heads down and pencils in hand, writing and writing as though it were as natural as taking a breath. Before, in Jamaica, we could *never.* What was the rule?

First form in Kingston. Twenty-four wooden desks in tidy rows, their tops etched with inscriptions from students past. In the top right corner of every desk were sinkholes for inkpots turned into waste bins for forbidden gum. The teacher paced at the front of the room, passing textbooks down the rows. *Algebra I. Introduction to Biology. Shakespeare's Tragedies.* Heavy books. Old books. Books with smiling white faces beneath layers of laminate, passed down through the years and kept pristine. These were Tamika's books, then my books, would have been Bryson's books, same editions passed on and on, no money to buy new every year. So what was the rule?

"Don't ever write in the books," I mumbled to myself.

"Um, hello?" Barrett said. "Earth to, uh—"

"Ak-Akua?" Sara said, coming close.

I looked up.

"Yeah, hi, good to have you back," Barrett said, scribbling something else in his book.

They used pencils so they could erase it later. They must. They *must*.

"Did you hear me?" Barrett said. "You're Santa Anna."

Blinking, I scanned the passage. "Who's Santa Anna?"

Sara looked at me, gaze blank. I puckered my lips in an exaggerated, *Who?*

"Head of the Mexican army," she said.

I scratched my head, feigning confusion.

"The bad guy," she said.

Barrett pointed at me then made that motion, *pu-kyiou.*

"Who am I gonna be?" asked Sara.

"Narrator," Barrett said, turning the page.

Sara crossed her arms. "Why am *I* the narrator?"

"'Cause," Barrett said.

"'Cause what?"

"'Cause you smell funny."

"Five minutes," Sister Marlene announced.

Sara sniffed her armpits. "I do *not* smell funny." She looked at me. "Do I?"

Running my hand over my hair, I gave a quick shrug.

Sara watched my hand pass over my cornrows. "What's in your hair?" she asked. "Like, what's that style?" She leaned forward, her palm under her chin.

"Cornrows." She didn't understand me, so I said it again. This time she watched me, her lips moving in sync with mine.

"Cornrows?" she said, squinting at the crisscrossing pattern. "Why are they called *cornrows*?"

"I, um," I scratched my neck. "I don't actually know." I'd never thought about it before.

"Cornrows," she repeated as she grabbed the end of a braid then let go.

"They're real."

She looked at my lips.

I yanked on a braid. "Real."

Smiling, she traced her fingers along each plait.

"How does it stay like that?" she said. "Like, so close to your head?" She pulled on a braid to bring my head a bit closer. "Are they supposed to look like corn?" She propped her feet on her chair then stretched across her desk toward me. "Do they hurt? They look like they hurt."

I let out a small laugh as she kept roving, taking it all in. "Yuh too fass', yuh 'no."

Sara leaned back, her hands flying from my hair.

"Was that Mexican?" Barrett whispered.

"Spanish!" Sara snapped.

Sister Marlene glared at us from across the room.

"Sorry," Sara muttered as she settled back into her chair and looked down at my hair oil coating her hands.

"Beeswax." I smiled at her. "That's how they stay."

She rubbed her fingers together, small curls of my hair caught under her nails.

"It's the beeswax that keeps them plaited tight," I said.

She sniffed her palms then wrinkled her nose.

"Smells funny, but—"

"Gross," she said, "so gross." She smeared the wax across the front of her backpack then used the straps to clean between her fingers.

I touched her elbow. "Sara?"

She opened her book then grabbed her pencil. Head down, she ignored me and pulled the lead across the page, scribbling, scribbling, just like everybody else.

"Go on, now, go on," Sister Marlene urged at the end of the exercise. "Your turn," she said.

Me and Barrett and Sara, we stood at the front of the room, all posed and dramatic like the little men on the swath of green.

At the end, fall on the floor, Barrett had told me.

But in the painting—

Just do it, Barrett had said. *Just fall. It'll look better.*

But in the painting in our textbooks, Santa Anna's standing, facing the white man on the ground—he's standing tall. But Barrett kept saying, *Just do it*, wouldn't let it go, *just fall*. So, at the end, I fell to the floor with Barrett standing over me, as Barrett said it should be, as the story next to the painting said it should be. Using the rubber end of my pencil, I pretended to sign the treaty as Sara narrated the surrender.

"Remember the Alamo!" Barrett yelled. *Pu-kyiou, pu-kyiou.*

And I lay there, muttering so only I could hear: *I say no I say no.*

Later, as we packed up our bags and waited for the period to end, Sister Marlene called to me. "Dear." She sat down, the chair creaking under her weight. "I need to know something," she said. "Tomorrow we have Mass, like we do every Thursday. So just to be sure," she leaned closer, "what religion are you?"

"I'm, uh—" I could smell peanuts and onions and something spicy on her breath. "I'm Anglican."

She knotted her brow. "What?"

"An.gli.can."

"Oh." She patted my wrist and laughed. "Episcopalian."

What?

"That's what we call you here," she said, bobbing her head after every other word. "When people ask, say, 'Episcopalian.'"

"Episco—*what?*" I stared at her, confused. "I'm Anglican." I puckered my lips and flailed my hands so she understood. *"Anglican."*

She got up. "Episcopalian, dear," she said. "For when people ask."

"She says she's Anglican," Sara chimed in.

Sister Marlene turned around.

"That's, that's what she, if you couldn't—" Sara gestured to my mouth.

Barrett was standing next to her, trying to smother a smile.

I said it again. "I'm Anglican."

"She's Anglican," Sara said, watching my lips.

"I was born Anglican."

"She was born Anglican."

"Christened Anglican—"

"Christened Anglican."

"My father is Anglican. My mother. My brother. How can you—*Episcopalian?* I'm Anglican!"

Barrett laughed. "Holy hell."

"That's what I am!" I beat my fists against my thighs. "That's what I *am*! You asked me and I told you!"

Sara looked at me, stunned. "Uh." She bit her bottom lip. "I didn't catch all that."

"An-gli-can," I repeated, nice and slow and bobbing my head after every syllable.

Barrett chuckled, laughing louder.

"An-gli-can," I sneered.

"Detention," Sister Marlene hissed.

Barrett doubled over as he laughed.

"Why?" Sara said, squinting up at Sister Marlene.

"An-gli-can," Barrett said, still giggling.

Sara pointed at me. "Y'asked her somethin'—"

"An-gli-can," Barrett repeated, louder this time, a few people joining in.

"—and she answered. I mean, I just." Sara paused, looking away.

"An-gli-can!" Barrett yelled, leading the chorus. He pointed his index finger and flexed his thumb. *Pu-kyiou.*

Sister Marlene surveyed the room, taking in all of us stomping and yelling and firing into the air. "In-class suspension!" she said.

The room fell silent.

"Tomorrow morning," she yelled. "I have never, I have *never*—" She stopped short. "No one is allowed to leave this room until I return with your blue slips." She looked at me. "Understand?"

As she turned to leave, I stood on my chair and gestured toward the closing door. *Pu-kyiou.*

I look down at my forefinger and thumb. *Pu-kyiou.* I'm sitting in my sister's apartment in Kingston, pushing my braids up and off my face. We're having breakfast. Tamika chews her cereal, avoiding my gaze. I want to tell her about Barrett, about being called Episcopalian when I'd told them I'm Anglican, that I insisted on who I knew myself to be. But I can't. I don't know how. There is no sweetness here, no easy conversation we can slip into like sisters should. Tamika picks at her nails as I reach for the milk. *What you did with that girl was wrong*, she said, but I am twenty now and I am not falling, I am not signing my surrender. Beneath the table, I knock my fists against my knees. *Les-bi-an.* Tamika sighs, already exhausted, so she gets up and turns the TV on.

The screen flashes fuzzy then settles on a football match, the announcer's voice booming through.

"Who's playing?" I ask.

"Brazil versus," Tamika squints to read the small words scrolling across the bottom of the screen, "Paraguay, I think?"

My sister does not like football, yet she turns her whole body toward the TV, intent on the game. I pour some cereal into my bowl, watching her chew.

"Where did *soccer* come from?" I ask as I drown my cereal in warm milk.

"What?" Tamika says.

"Like, the word." I cough. "How did *football* become *soccer*?"

Tamika sighs. "Mi nuh know, sah."

Nodding, I spoon some cereal into my mouth. The TV pops with garbled shouts, something raucous and angry—a red card on the green.

"Kinda reminds me of when people say ackee tastes like scrambled eggs," I tell her.

Tamika screws up her face.

"That's what people say." That's what Sara said the first time she tried it. "People abroad, I mean. They say it tastes like scrambled eggs."

The noise from the TV swells as someone moves in for a goal.

"Is wha kinda foolishness dat?" Tamika says.

I smirk. "Mi nuh know, sah."

She chuckles then tenses as the first half of the game draws to a close. I stare at my bowl, at the bloated circles floating in tepid white. Tamika can sense it, knows the soccer and ackee are a prelude, the earthy sweetness that comes before a deluge. *Why didn't you come for me? Why won't you see me?* I set my spoon down in my bowl.

"Where will you go today?" Tamika says.

"What?"

She closes the milk. "You should go down by Half Way Tree," she says. "It's nice there now, different from what you remember."

My spoon slips lower into my cereal. "You're letting me go?"

Tamika rubs the bridge of her nose, then throws her napkin down in surrender. A TV jingle starts up, breaking the tense silence—*QuenchAid is my number one.* She sighs, pushing her bowl away in a seeming *Yes. I'm tired. So go.* I stare at her, jaw slack.

Tamika gestures to the front door then says, "Good luck."

WEDNESDAY

18 Days Left

I'M STANDING OUTSIDE MY SISTER'S APARTMENT with my brother in my backpack, taking care to lock then dead-bolt the door before bounding down the stairs. Opening the lobby door, I glance back. I can hear loud banging and scraping from Tamika rummaging around in her living room. This is what I wanted. I'm going out alone. Lingering on the lobby threshold, I hear a sharp thud then *shhhh* of Tamika dragging something across the floor. I keep gazing up the stairs, willing the door to open and my sister to walk through. My body turns toward her hard sounds as the spring in the door clicks, nudging me outside. She's not coming. Thrusting my hand into my backpack, I check that my brother's still tucked away safe. It is a perfectly windless day.

Traffic streams down the two-lane road, Suzukis with mismatched bumpers and pickup trucks carrying bushels of fresh cane. There's foot traffic too, men in polos with sweat darkening their spines next to women in cropped jeans and sandals turning red with dirt. They chat as they walk, their legs moving as slow as their mouths. But they're moving at least, they know where they're going. I fix my face and set my mind on where I'm going too. I want to go to Half Way Tree. I want to walk up Constant Spring Road. I want to go to King Street—is it still called King Street? All I remember are cream buildings with tall columns lining the black tar road that leads straight to the sea. Adjusting the straps of my backpack, I close my eyes and hold my brother close. This is what I wanted. I make myself move.

I pass a group of high school girls out for lunch on my way to the bus stop. Glancing at their tunics and pleated skirts, I feel the tug of something I should know. The girls line up in front of a food cart, curls springing loose from their slicked-back buns as a city bus pulls up just ahead. I manage to squeeze on before the doors snap shut. A bus going where? I don't know. I find a spot near a window and watch the girls talking and joking as they buy their food, the bus pulling into the easy-moving traffic.

We pass town houses and a depot store, its blue banner sagging in the hot hot sun. Wild goats munch on patches of weeds next to shops closed up behind zinc shutters, graffiti scrawled on top. Weaving through a roundabout, we pull over next to a primary school, three squat buildings painted brown and beige. Boys in dirty khakis and girls in pink dresses come running toward the bus and I remember! I don't know where I'm going but I know where I've been. I remember staring at myself in the bathroom mirror, at my own brown tunic with pleats starched crisp. First day of first form. I was ten years old.

Gray light slanted in through the shutters, coloring the high school auditorium in a sleepy haze. Blinking, I looked about, smelling hair oil and clothes starch in the early morning heat. I was standing in my first form line, which was next to second form, which was next to third, fourth, fifth, all of us arranged in neat rows facing the low stage. My eyes on the headmistress, I reached toward the girl in front, tracing letters across the brown fabric on her back. We were passing notes, drawing the letters one by one, messages sent through the quiet of touch. *We are good girls*, our headmistress said, *smart girls*. We must affirm our devotion to eternal salvation before turning to matters of the mind. Rubbing my eyes, I stifled a deep yawn.

The headmistress led us through prayer then snapped her Bible shut, signaling for everyone to join together, reciting as one: *The Lord is my shepherd. I shall not want.* At the close of the psalm, the teachers broke formation to lead the way to the exits. Pinching and shoving, we followed behind in clumps of jostling brown. Someone snickered, pointing at a girl just ahead with pink bubbles in her hair. Her skirt was bunched up in her bloomers, showing two birthmarks jiggling on the back of her thigh. I laughed along with everyone else but clamped my left hand around my right wrist, tight like cuffs against the desire to run my fingers along her bare skin. I watched the pouring rain through the window and wondered what Anancy first called this feeling when he spun his web round and round.

The bus lurches forward. We pass a mall—RED HILLS MALL, the sign says—as one-story plazas become two- and three-. The bars and corner shops become dentist offices and travel agencies as we get closer to downtown. The bus takes a corner fast with tires squealing, pedestrians watching us careen past then come to a sudden stop.

A woman around my age gets on wearing too-tight jeans with Lady Saw echoing through the headphones around her neck. She's short and curvy, a long scar down her shoulder shining waxy in the afternoon light. "Excuse," she says, her hips brushing against mine as she squeezes past.

We pass higglas perched under umbrellas, bags of cut pineapple and peppa shrimp laid out on strips of tarp. I look back at the girl. She's dark-skinned and lovely, chest barely contained by her pink tube top. She cotches on an aisle seat and crosses her left leg over her right, the top of her hip spilling over into the flitting sunlight. Cuffing my right hand with my left, I exhale slow, tasting guinep.

The bus driver leans on his horn, yelling at the taxi that just cut him off. The windows in the bus are all closed. The taxi driver can't hear him. The bus driver keeps yelling anyway, riding the taxi's bumper straight through to the next light.

"Is what dat, man?" the woman listening to Lady Saw says. "Him sure him know how fi drive?"

I glance back at her again, guinep flooding my tongue. As

we round a cawna, the bus stops to pick up more passengers. Everyone squeezes closer together, making space.

"Lawd Jesus," someone at the back exclaims, "yuh tek we fi sardine?"

The bus driver peers into the rearview mirror. "Den tek yuh two long leg and galang 'bout yuh business!" he says.

First one then two people then the whole bus erupts in air sucked through dead-set teeth. The bus driver revs the engine, pulling back onto the road. I can still glimpse the woman between shoulders and over backpacks. She has her headphones over her ears now, gaze gone soft and music turned all the way up. I try catching her eye with a smile. She doesn't see me, keeps bobbing her head to the beat. She doesn't need to see me. She's probably as straight as they come. Sighing, I rest my head against the cool railing, wishing for Sara as we move down the potholed road.

Teenagers on bicycles wind between the lanes of traffic, young boys standing on the back axle and others sitting between the handlebars like swaddled children. My brother never learned how to ride a bicycle. I was supposed to teach him but I couldn't, because I'd never learned either. Leaning over, I ring the bell to get off.

"One stop, driva," I yell.

He overtakes a JUTA bus, paying me no mind.

"Mi seh one stop!" I exclaim.

More people pull on the bell, filling the bus with tinny *ding-ding*s.

"Nuh bruk mi bell!" the driver says as he pulls onto the shoulder and finally lets us off.

Standing on the grassy bank, I watch people streaming into the market and clothes shops and post office across the street. There's a clock tower nearby, cream walls with blue base and a small bellhouse on top. Behind it are billboard after billboard, ads for Mother's restaurants and CheeZees snacks bearing down on the traffic below. So this is Cross Roads.

Bryson loved CheeZees but never got a chance to eat at Mother's. He barely remembered leaving Kingston, his hand slapping blissful against the sides of his car seat. For him, that first move was a thrilling adventure—like a great big game of *now you see it, now you don't.* When Daddy sat us down in Texas and told us we were moving again, Bryson beamed up at me, stupid and free. He thought the move to Canada would be just as happy. How could I tell him? He was older by then, almost six. How could I let him know? This time, he would remember. This time, he would feel the whole hurt.

Three weeks after Daddy told us, we packed up and sold the house in Texas. I remember watching Bryson, his eyes wide and unblinking as he stood in the departures lounge looking at the bright signs on tall walls with letters flipping—NOW BOARDING FLIGHT 544 FLIGHT 698 TO FORT LAUDERDALE DELAYED NEW ARRIVAL TIME FOR FLIGHT 3636 GATE FOR FLIGHT 643 CHANGED CAROUSEL FOR FLIGHT 566 CHANGED NOW BOARDING NOW DEPARTING—

"Bryson," Daddy called. "Come nuh, man."

Bryson pretended not to hear. Heels pressed into the tile

floor, he looked at the men rushing and children crying and mothers fussing then he looked at me, the truth setting in.

"Where are we going?" he said. "Why do we have to leave?"

Daddy had told us where we were going but we had never heard of it, couldn't picture it, Vancouver as real to us as the inside of the moon.

I pulled my brother to me, burying his face in my shirt. Daddy moved up in the security line toward the guard waving his long wand in loud *cracklecracklebeeps*. I held my brother, his heels stacked on my toes and face pressed against my stomach till he couldn't hear the letters flipping or wand crackling, just the smooth thump of my beating heart. I carried him because this is what you do. I balanced my brother's feet on mine because when your sibling is hurting, you carry them and you walk them through. The man circled us with his wand once, twice.

"Is he special?" the security guard whispered, gesturing to my brother.

I said nothing, just stared straight ahead and walked us forward. After a few minutes, we cleared security and Bryson walked next to me, arms around my waist, as we found our gate. He wouldn't let go of me until we got to the new house. Daddy heaved heavy boxes onto the front porch, forehead sweaty and sleeves rolled up. No movers that time, no palm trees drooping against black fence—just us and the crisp Pacific air. Bryson looked around his new room, his eyes bloodshot and pleading.

"So," he sputtered, "so is this it?"

I pressed my hand against his back. "Yes."

"I hate it," he said as he picked at a wad of packing paper, his small shoulders shaking.

I rubbed his back. "I know."

"This place is weird." He ripped the paper to pieces. "Their cops are called Mounties. *Mounties.* That doesn't make me scared. That makes me laugh. Ha! Ha! Ha!" He slumped against my chest, his snot dribbling onto my sleeve. "I hate it, I hate it, I hate it!" he screamed, beating his fists against my sides.

"What are you, baby Tarzan?"

He let out a snot-nosed laugh. "I want to go home," he mumbled.

Home. I held him.

Home. I'm standing on the grassy bank at Cross Roads, holding him still. Tamika didn't come up to help us with the move. It was just me and him, him and me. Wiping my forehead with my shirtsleeve, I look at the people coming and going. CROSS ROADS MARKET, the wrought-iron sign says, arched above an entryway clogged with Corollas. I can hear higglas bartering amid music blasting with too much bass. My body shifts toward the thumping vibrations, drawn to the crush of bodies—black, black, dark like me.

All around me are wooden stalls covered in handbags and T-shirts and white socks and mesh caps and suitcases boasting NIKKE and PRADO. Mothers haggle over sneaker prices as girls skipping school pick through bottles of knock-off perfume. Burly men push past me carrying boxes full of things—heavy things, bulky things, some wrapped in newspaper and others in strips of plastic as an old woman whacks me in the calves with her cane. I'm blocking the opening of an aisle.

"Which flava yuh want?" a girl says to me, waving her arm over the cooler of bag juice for sale.

The old woman whacks my leg again. Sliding to the left to let her pass, I glance at the frozen lumps radiating cold steam. Neon green. Neon purple. Artificially bright and sickly sweet. Pulling on the straps of my bag, I try to imagine which flavor Bryson would've liked.

"I'll go with orange," I tell the girl.

She drops the lump in my hand along with my change. Bryson loved tangerines, peaches. Orange would've been his flavor, even though they all taste the same. Biting off the corner, I chew the icy sweetness until it breaks up into a sticky slush. Inhaling deep, I smell vegetables musty with fresh earth and skin scrubbed clean with castile soap. The crowd thickens as I near the back of the building, trying to imagine what else in this market Bryson might've liked.

He would've liked the T-shirts, maybe even the cheap shoes. He had a thing for graphic tees with bright sneakers. On another higgla's table, there are dolls and puzzles and miniature model cars. Would he like the small red and purple cars, HOT WHEELZ emblazoned on their sides? Staring into an aisle, I try to imagine that higgla a likkle more to de left, and dat customer a likkle more to the right, making just enough room for a Bryson-shaped space. I chew and chew till my gums go numb.

"'Ello," a higgla calls, waving a basket in my face. "Look pon missus a jus' march 'round wid two long eye. Come buy sum'n nuh!"

Shaking my head no, I make to move on.

"Weh yuh from?" she says, stopping me again.

I try to ignore her but she waves the basket again, blocking my way. She has bowls—big bowls, skinny bowls, wide and shallow bowls awaiting papayas and naseberries and East Indian mangoes. She has vases with fat bottoms and skinny necks painted red and gold, and bowler hats and cowboy hats fashioned from banana leaves, fronds sticking out in makeshift fringe.

"Yuh from foreign?" she says.

I step a little closer. The hats and bowls, they have no lacquer, the edges of the hats already browning from the dank market air. I imagine them offering a day's worth of shade then adorning someone's mantel, a dry and brittle keepsake above a crackling foreign fire.

"Yuh have nuff bredda an' sista?" she says. "Nice souvenir dis." She pushes a figurine into my hand. It's a hummingbird with toothpicks for feet and a body fatter than my hand.

"Ten dolla," she says.

Smirking, I look up at her. "Ten dollars Jamaican?"

She laughs. "Naw, sah. Ten dolla Jamaican cyaa even buy mi wah degge degge cocobread." She pushes another trinket into my hand. Daddy likes hummingbirds. I should call him soon.

"Five dollars," I tell her, holding on to the small bird.

"Eight," she says.

"Five." Throwing away my bag juice, I open my wallet. "And I'm not paying you in American."

"Is what dat?" She points at my wallet. "Yuh carry 'round a wallet like wah man?" I can hear the nastiness in her voice.

"I'm not a man." I take out my cash. That's what I said to Bryson when I bought the wallet. *I'm not a man.* He thumbed the stiff leather then said, *I know.*

The higgla's eyes twitch faster. "Are you strange?" she hisses.

"Strange how?"

She points to my wallet. "Yuh a walk 'round with wah wallet—"

"And wha wrong wid dat?" I cut in. "So me must carry purse for thief fi come grab it so?"

She chuckles as she hears me speak. "Is whe yuh live now?" she says. "Mus' be 'Merica."

"Nuh pay har no mind, yuh hear?" another higgla says. "De woman too fasty fi har own good." They look at each other then laugh, a deep sort of laugh, passing knowing looks with me shut out and confused. I drop the bird on the table then walk to the other higgla, pretending to understand.

"How yuh do?" she says.

"So so," I respond, like I heard my sister say in Mathews Lane.

Paying in Canadian, I buy a bun and cock soup. I don't even know what to do with cock soup, but I hear the sharp inhale of the other woman and smile to myself as I take my purchases then leave. Edging my way through the crowd, I hear the two women fighting, quarreling over who should've gotten that sale.

Hordes of people move between the two buildings, munching on patties and roast peanuts while belching smoke from thin cigarettes. I tear a hole in the plastic bag then break off a piece of bun. The dense bread sticks to the roof of my mouth, sweet and comforting like a familiar surprise. It needs cheese. I remember now. Bun should be sliced open, a thick layer of Tastee cheese sandwiched inside. Bryson loved Tastee cheese.

"Akúa?" my brother said. He was seven.

"Yes, little man?"

"Do we have any cheese?" he said, holding a slice of bun in his hand. The bun was stale and slightly graying from the two weeks spent in the mail from Jamaica to Canada.

"I'm sorry, little man." I shook my head no.

He sighed, biting into the dry bun. "We match," he said, tugging on my pants hanging from the door hook. At school, they gave us the choice between knee-length skirts or khaki pants for our uniform. I grabbed the pants faster than I could understand. Yes, pants. I didn't know why yet, but pants.

"I'm gonna wear fun socks," I told Bryson.

He smiled. "Me too."

"I'll do purple."

"I'll do red!" he said, hurrying down the hall to finish getting dressed.

Half hour later, we hopped in the car, already ten minutes late for homeroom. At school in Canada, one girl asked me to sit with her, to tell her about my country's foods and how to make them. No, I told her. Another asked me my name and where I was from. I didn't respond. They were much nicer than Texans, I'll give them that, much calmer and gentler about discovering all the ways I wasn't like them. But still, I shoved my hands in my pockets and kept my mouth shut.

Standing in the market at Cross Roads, I take my hands out of my pockets and squeeze my backpack to feel my brother inside. Was that how my sister felt when we moved to Texas, shipped to a new land that she didn't choose so she closed herself up, keeping herself distant and safe?

"Fresh coconut wata!" a man yells, grabbing coconuts from the pile in his truck bed. He chops off the tops then empties the water into old milk jugs. "Two hundred. Nice price, dat," he says, holding out a coconut to my prying eyes. Music blasts from his truck's speakers as he chops then pours, chops then pours. *Rememba de days*, the speakers echo, treble warbling through the old wires.

"Mi cyaa hear yuh," a higgla says as she leans across boxes of onions and bananas, pumpkins stacked by her feet.

"How much?" a woman asks her, fresh sap seeping from the green banana in her arms.

The car stereo struggles as the volume goes up. *We coulda party till de sunrise* as up and down the narrow rows, people start to move to the beat *wid no fear o' being victimized*. A few people sing along as they count coins then hand back change.

"*And our love woulda neva cease* but nuh squeeze up, squeeze up mi fruits dem, man," a higgla sneers, shooing a man away. "Yuh hand dem big like gorilla, Jesus!"

Pushing farther into the crowd, I pass tables of scallion and callaloo next to mounds of green cherries as *when peace an' love was de orda of de day* rolls over women hawking gungo peas and passion fruit and it feels less hot, not quite as sweltering, as I squeeze next to bodies burning with the need to sing. *Let's live in love an' harmony* as the smell of sweetsop fills me till wanting and I'm singing too. I'm standing in the middle, happily drowning in the crush of us all. *Mi believe in every word she say* as I squeeze through to a woman selling overripe Bombays and spotted number threes.

"Two hundred fi six," she says.

I buy three, mouth still sticky from the dry bun, remembering an old trick. Crouching down, I knock a Bombay against a rock, taking care not to break the skin. Two, four, five times, *bangbang*, until I feel the mango turn soft as Jell-O. Biting a small hole in the skin, I suck out the sweet flesh. Mango juice, no tools required. Tamika taught me this trick one summer when she stole some mangoes from the neighbor's tree down the road. I should've taught it to Bryson before he died.

Bending down, I unzip my bag then squeeze mango juice into my hand. Flying the latch, I reach into his box and sprinkle a bit of him on top, making a slurry between my palms. I wait until the song reaches another crescendo. I wait until there's no one watching and then I smear him on a rock, on a tree, on the side of a higgla's table when she's turned her back to make change. I smear him on a coconut, on a van, on the metal grate of the speakers still blasting the sweet song. Welcome home, Bryson. I smear him everywhere like he's here too.

Someone throws a rock at my back. Turning around, I see the woman from the bus, Lady Saw echoing from the headphones in her hand. She's watching me, a strange look on her face. Before she can say anything, I close up my brother in my bag and I run.

THURSDAY

17 Days Left

I T'S MORNING. MY SHEETS LAY CRUMPLED AT the base of my bed. This is how you bear it: in the quiet of night, without moving and without waking, sense the wane of the crickets buzzing and tree frogs chirping as they give way to rising light—then kick the covers off, free yourself of the top sheet before the birds wake and morning heat starts seeping in. This is how, here, at home, you get a good night's sleep.

Yawning, I stretch and scratch my stomach. My shorts and socks are still dry, my tank top just shy of damp. Eyes open, I reach above my bed to press my palm against the windowpane. It is smooth and hot, glass rattling with the bass riddim from a passing car.

"Come eat!" Tamika yells.

I drop my hand. Did our mother call us like that? I close my eyes, trying to conjure her: face like Bryson like Tamika like me, standing in our old house, in our living room or kitchen. I squeeze my eyes shut and think and think but all I see is darkness. I throw my legs over the side of my bed. Walking into the kitchen, I hold up the plastic bag for Tamika to see.

"I bought mangoes," I announce.

Tamika nods, chewing her toast at the kitchen table. I put the mangoes in the wooden bowl next to the yellow yam.

"Remember that trick you taught me?" I shape my hand into a lopsided O. "I bought a Bombay, ripest one in the box, then I found a rock—not a sharp one, a smooth one—and then," *knock knock knock*, I bang my hand against warm air, *knock knock knock*, I move my hand in the smooth motion to show her I still understand.

Tamika smiles then touches my arm. "I have a surprise for you," she says then points to a warped cardboard box on the living room settee.

There's a netball and old binders spread across the floor, the smell of mothballs rising like nostalgia and death. There are sun-bleached posters, empty pill bottles, a stack of VHS tapes in a neat pile next to the TV. This was all the banging I heard yesterday.

"Sit down," she says.

I'm curious, so I sit. Tamika pops a tape into the VCR as I set my backpack between my feet.

"*Is long time gyal mi neva see yuh,*" Miss Lou sings, "*come mek mi hol' your hand.*" Tamika sits next to me as the band starts up, unruly and glorious. She watches me, smiling. We're watching *Ring Ding* like I would with our mother when I was young.

"*Is a long time gyal mi neva see yuh, come mek mi hol' your *hand,"* Miss Lou sings. *"Peel-head John Crow sit 'pon di treetop, pick out di blossom, let me hol' your hand."*

My hands clench. "Who's John Crow?"

"A vulture," Tamika says.

"Ah," I respond, still mystified but watching just the same. My empty stomach rumbles with remnants of dry bulla.

"I'm sorry," Tamika says, "for stealing the tapes. And for, for—" She twirls her hand around and around in the empty air then takes my arm, rubbing my wrist with her thumb.

"For what?" I ask her.

Her smile cracks.

"Sorry for what?" My cheeks go flush as my palms turn cold. Balling my hands into hard fists, I sit on them, crushing this old anger till my fingers start to hurt.

On-screen Miss Lou spins, children dancing all around her. The picture blips and starts to scroll up, splicing Miss Lou in half so that her stomach is near the top of the TV and her head just beneath her shuffling feet. I hunch my shoulders and squeeze my elbows against my ribs to keep my body steady, everything rigid against the burning need to scream.

I was so angry when I realized Tamika took the tapes. Daddy and I had just come home from our new church in Texas. *Episcopalian* is the church we'd gone to, even though we were Anglican. Daddy didn't care. He took me to church out of habit, because that was what my mother would have done if she were there. As I changed out of my church clothes and made myself a snack, I looked around the strange house, searching for some sign of what I once knew. I wanted my tapes. I wanted to lose myself in whatever wily scheme Anancy was spinning next.

"Do you know where Daddy put the Miss Lou tapes?" I asked Tamika when she finally picked up the phone.

"Tell Daddy to send the rest of my school fee," she said, two weeks into her first term at Hampton.

"Tell him yuhself," I huffed. "Where are the tapes?"

"Jus' tell him nuh," she said. "Why yuh a give me all dis boderation?"

Down the hall, I heard Bryson waking from his nap. "Tell me where they are," I murmured, slow and threatening, "or else I'm putting Daddy on the phone."

Bryson's squeals turned to cries as I heard Daddy cross the hall toward his crib. I could hear Tamika breathing hard.

"Daddy!" I yelled, the receiver pressed against my cheek.

"*Akúa*," Tamika hissed.

Daddy held up his hand, signaling he'd be there soon.

"Daddy!" I yelled again.

"Akúa, stop!" she said.

"Daaaaddy!"

"How yuh so stupid?" Tamika sneered. "Cyaa see simple two plus two," she said. "I took them."

I stopped yelling as she started laughing.

"I took them, I took them, *I took them*," she hissed, voice sharp as a barb, then she hung up.

I heard Daddy next to me, asking what she wanted. I ignored him and called her back, listening to the phone ring and ring then click over to voice mail. So I called again, then again, and

Daddy sighed, from far away I heard him sigh then walk away as I called again, and again, hanging up as soon as the voice mail clicked on then pressing 876 to call again until I got her back, until I had my tapes, and I dialed again until she came back yelling, "*What?*"

"When are you sending them back?"

"When I visit," Tamika said.

"When are you coming to visit?"

"Why would I visit?"

"Because you just said—"

"So stupid," she said, chuckling.

I banged the phone against the wall. She kept laughing, unafraid.

"Talk to me, then," I yelled, my chest thumping hard.

"What?"

I couldn't have Miss Lou or my mother or the house I called home so, "Talk to me," I said again.

Church was done and there we were, my sister and me, on the phone. This would be my Sunday school, I decided. This would be my holy education.

"Uh," Tamika stammered then hung up.

I called her back, my fingers poised over 876.

"Jeezam peez," she said, "how yuh so stubborn? Come in jus' like mosquito."

"I learned from you."

She kissed her teeth.

"Please talk to me," I murmured.

The wind picked up on her side. I imagined her leaning

against a wall, one hand on her hip and left knee popped forward, jutting and defiant and alone. She sighed. "I cut open a frog today," she said.

"Ew."

"We started dissections in lab."

"Oh."

"They were messy. Really messy. And dem smell like wha! But is a'right. I did my cuts and took my notes. I have PE tomorrow. I love netball—"

"Me too!" I exclaimed.

"I know," she said. "Who do you think taught you how to play? So anyway, my PE teacher is the devil. She starts every block with a lecture about cutting our nails, especially the ones in our shoes. On and on about them for ten, twenty minutes. Why does she care so much about our toenails? That's not normal."

I chuckled.

"One of my classmates got detention yesterday," she said. "She's the first person to get detention in two years. Mi friend dem started a bet to see how long until she gets expelled. We had snapper for dinner last night. I think they forgot to take off the scales, de skin come in tough like bulla."

"Daddy took me to a park yesterday," I exclaimed. "No one there knew about netball. They played some other game, something called a double dutch. It looked like fun but I didn't get it."

"Did you ask them to explain?" she said.

"Well, I *asked*, but then, I don't know, yeah, I asked—"

"Next time," she said, "push your way in. Nuh pay no mind if anybody try block yuh out. Keep doing it until you get it. Just try."

Exhaling, I nodded as if she could see.

"We're going on a field trip next week," she said. "Somewhere on the north coast. I don't care where we're going. I just hope we get KFC."

She filled the phone with stories about the city bus that was always late and the fight that broke out after the football match at the school down the street as I clutched the receiver close, warming my hands with her racket. My body curled toward the heat of her voice as I sat alone inside the cold and foreign house.

Now I'm in her apartment in Kingston and her voice brings me no warmth. Tamika's sitting next to me on the couch, nodding along to the beat of Miss Lou's song. I glance at her as I squeeze my elbows harder against my ribs. Her hair grazes her cheek and I imagine turning fast, throwing my whole weight behind my fist to feel her chin give way. The tapes were all I had of my mother, and she took them. I stop sitting on my hands then crack my knuckles one by one.

"Long time now mi neva see yuh, come mek we wheel an' turn," Miss Lou sings, taking a young girl by the hand and spinning her around. "Now, that is the Jamaican mento song. I welcome you, so now you will welcome me. Sing wid me now!" Miss Lou starts down the aisle, arms outstretched to every person she passes.

I rub the back of my hand, skin buzzing electric.

"Come mek mi hol' your hand," the crowd sings to her. *"Long time now mi neva see yuh, come mek mi hol' your hand."*

"We were young, y'know?" Tamika says. "I don't know why I took them. Just the stupid games kids play."

My insides churn with a hotness roiling deep. I want to hurt her. I want her to see what happens when all she does is take. Tamika stands up.

"I'm going to church tomorrow," she says then turns toward the hall. Tomorrow evening, like all propa Jamaican women do, she will disappear into the bathroom, water hot and cleansing. She will rifle through her drawer full of pantyhose until she finds a white pair that has no runs. She will iron her dress and powder her forehead and nose. Then she will reappear in sling-back heels with a small purse over one shoulder, Jovan Musk wafting from her neck. She will stand with her shoulders back and spine dead-straight. She will look like a good and holy woman.

I force my fists open, flattening my palms against my thighs. "I'm coming with you," I mumble.

She rolls her eyes. She knows I hate church. I swallow the bile collecting at the back of my throat. I could hit her—and then? I think of Daddy outside her door, beating the lacquered wood till his fist turned ketchup red. And then? She receded, sunk beneath the surface, leaving me lost and stricken waiting onshore. We are sisters, not friends.

Standing up, I sling my backpack over my shoulder then turn the TV off. I look around her apartment as she glances down at my pants.

"You didn't even bring one skirt fi church?" she says.

Clenching my jaw, I gesture for her to lead. Ladies first.

FRIDAY

16 Days Left

THE CHOIR STANDS AS A YOUNG MAN TAKES the mic. "Let us give thanks," he says, "to the sweet Lord, our Jesus." He closes his eyes, raising his hands into the air. "Merciful Jesus, our God and Savior." He moves side to side in time with the piano. "He died for our sins, so let us praise Him."

"Praise Him!" someone yells.

"Let us bring glory to His name," the young man says.

"Glory, hallelujah!"

"Forget your worries and earthly concerns. Give yourself to Him."

"Yes, Lord!"

"Lift your hands and worship Him for this joy we have that the world cannot take away."

The congregation rises, turning their palms toward the ceiling as they start to sing. We're sitting in the third pew from the front, Tamika in an orange chiffon dress and me in chinos and a blue polo. There's a couple next to us, the husband in a stiff white button-down and his wife in a yellow blazer with shoulder pads as thick as my wrist.

The couple and the whole congregation—they're on their feet and they're singing with such bombast, such flourish, faces shining with conviction, and this was a mistake. I'm standing and I'm moving my lips but I am not raising my arms in euphoric surrender. I am not bellowing till my throat grows hoarse. I watch as the congregation proclaims their devotion in fits of ecstatic splendor—devotion to what? I look around the room at dust flecks twinkling gray in the warm air. I glance at my sister and wonder if she knows, if everyone is in on the big lie but me. A woman steps forward from the choir then takes the mic from the young man.

"Praise Jesus!" Tamika exclaims, opening her arms to the overhead fans.

The singing swells as the woman begins her solo, the blue fascinator in her hair swaying with every trill of her voice. *Sing hallelujah to the Lord our God* as Tamika claps in time with the music. *Every praise, every praise, to our God* as Tamika watches the woman, gaze adoring. The choir rises in a smooth crescendo, the singers waving their hands as the pastor mounts the steps to the pulpit.

"Amen," everyone says then sits.

The pastor delivers his opening remarks as my pants turn damp with sweat like sitting in school chapel, muggy Texas heat collecting behind bored knees. I haven't been back to Texas since we left. Barrett still sends me cards at Christmas and Easter, little notes printed at the pharmacy with photos of his wife and two kids. Sara called him once and told him we were together. The three of us had been best friends for years. The line went dead, nothing to say.

The pastor calls for us to turn to scripture somethingsomething. I glance over as Tamika pulls her Bible from her purse, flipping the pages and nodding her head in silent conviction. My sister, dear sister. The pastor raises his arms, sunlight streaming in through the stained glass at the rear of the sanctuary.

"Lift your hands and worship Him," he says.

Everyone raises their hands again, palms turned bloody by the red tint from the image in the stained glass: their Lord in Gethsemane, white face turned yellow by searing sun.

I lean my shoulder against my sister's. "Tamika," I whisper, "why is Jesus white?"

"What?"

"Why is Jesus white?" I point at the stained glass. "Isn't he supposed to be from the Middle East?"

"It's stained glass, you idiot," she hisses. "He's see-through to let in the sun."

"Ah," I respond with a nod. Huffing, she smooths her hair then fixes her eyes on the pastor.

"Tamika," I whisper.

She ignores me.

"Tamika." I nudge her shoulder. "Why is Jesus see-through?"

"Stop it!" she hisses—but I see it, just barely, the corners of her lips curving into a small smile.

Pretending to fix my pants, I slide a little closer. She keeps facing forward, nodding along as the pastor expounds the glories of somethingoranother. Tamika, it's me. People clap and shout, "Yes, Lord!" as the pastor bellows on. Your baby sister. It's still me. Tamika joins them, lost in their fervor. Sighing, I give up and face the stained glass, the crest of our country embossed on the wall just below.

"Hallelujah!" the pastor exclaims as he leaves the pulpit and returns to his bench. "Let us pray."

I close my eyes and mime along: Our Father, who art in heaven, how are my mother and brother doing? The prayer ends as the pastor rises, bringing out the bowl of bread and chalice of juice. My sister remains as she is, head bent in prayer.

The pastor makes the sign of the cross over the food as the soloist steps forward, fascinator now in hand, and starts a new hymn. At the sound of her voice, Tamika looks up with an expression I can't explain. The choir rocks in time with the soloist scaling up and down in quick turns. Even as everyone lines up in the center aisle to meet the pastor, Tamika stays seated, still watching the soloist with that look, that look that says—! I want to crawl in through her ear and stand behind her eyes, just to see, to know.

A little girl nudges my leg. Moving to let her pass, I watch the green bubbles jiggle in her hair as she gets to Tamika. My sister blinks then stands as the girl skips past toward the line. I glance at the soloist, then at Tamika, then mouth a silent, *Who's she?* Tamika blinks, face empty, then leaves the pew. Another question; another silence. Groaning, I follow her up the aisle.

Tamika accepts her piece of bread and sip of juice from the pastor with a soft genuflection then makes the sign of the cross. I step forward as the pastor dips his hand back into the bowl.

"The body of Christ," he says, placing the stale bread on my lips. "The blood of Christ." The warm fluid floods my tongue. How many people's backwash did I just drink?

Tamika glares at me as I leave the line and link my hands behind my back. I know what she wants. She wants me to touch my forehead, my shoulders, and chest with the sign of their cross but I just keep walking. She grabs my arm as I pass her, gesturing to the sanctuary with her chin. Turning around, I look up at her see-through Jesus and I give him a hearty thumbs-up. Tamika kisses her teeth and marches back to our seats.

The thing is, I hate church—not on principle, but from years of overexposure. In primary school, here in Kingston, I started every weekday yawning my way through morning devotion in a stuffy auditorium. And then we moved, *a chance for everything to change!* Yet I ended up spending every Thursday from one thirty to three in mandatory school chapel at Catholic school in Texas. It seemed like church was as inescapable as breathing, so I learned how to hollow out. I taught myself how to make my legs stand when everyone around me stood and kneel when they knelt while my head floated off, swimming in a sea of its own making.

There was the time I was thirteen and Sara and I were in the eighth grade. "Middle school," they called it. It was a Thursday, chapel day. All around me were dark wooden pews crammed full of my classmates squirming in blue uniforms, sweat collecting in armpits and elbows. I closed my eyes, slipping into the warmth and safety of my dreams.

The water lapped up, licking my toes. I was four, maybe five, curled up in my father's arms as he carried me out to sea. The distant whir of an airplane engine drowned out the piercing squawk of swooping birds. My father's palm felt large, abrasive against my skin as he scooped up handfuls of salty water to cool my scorching back. Shutting my eyes tight, I wouldn't let go. I was a bad swimmer, such a bad swimmer, so I pressed my face against his neck and sucked the salt from my thumb. That was as close to the sea as I'd get. My father carried me around, wading through the water as I clung to him, my hand in my mouth as I sucked the sea in.

"Get up," Sara hissed in my ear.

In the school pulpit, the priest held the chalice above his head. A beeper sounded; someone laughed; *clack-clack* of black shoes against tile as a nun advanced to the sounding beeper. My stomach growled. I was hungry and it was time for Communion. Afterward, we joined hands and said the Lord's Prayer—same routine as the Thursday before, and the Thursday before.

"You shouldn't have done that," Sara said later as she trailed behind me.

Hands darted around shoulders and snuck between backpacks as everyone reached for the food laid out for sale on the white plastic table: breakfast taquitos and sausage biscuits and boxes of lukewarm juice. We were on "recess."

"Done what?" I dug through my pockets, fingers rubbing against an uncapped pen and bits of lint. "You got a five?"

"You shouldn't have taken Communion," Sara said.

"Make it a ten. You have a ten? I'm starving."

Sara crossed her arms. "Did you hear me?"

A boy laughed—loud, nasal, voice crackling with the first signs of growing up. A bunch of guys were standing on the other side of the courtyard poring over some magazine, the tallest leaning against the wooden cross by the wall. It was Barrett; that bastard still owed me five dollars. Sara grabbed my arm.

"Hmm?" I said to her.

She kept staring, unflinching.

"Yeah yeah, shouldn't have taken Communion." I turned around. "Why not?"

"Because you're not Catholic."

Arms out, I started shoving to find a place in the throng. "Well, you shouldn't listen to rap music."

"What?"

"Because you're not Black," I said.

"That's not the same thing."

Pushing forward, I could smell fried-black bacon and melted cheese wafting from the steaming taquitos.

"Seriously," Sara said.

"Shut up."

She grabbed my shirt. "You could go to hell for that."

Groaning, I faced her. She bit her lower lip, cheeks surging up in a smile.

"Whatever."

She burst out laughing.

Smirking, I wrapped my arm around her neck in one big poppyshow. "Now gimme all your lunch money!"

She giggled, pulling out a five. "Wait, doesn't Barrett or someone owe you money?"

I grabbed it—smiling, smiling.

Later, recess over and my stomach full of eggs and cheese, I closed my eyes and let myself drift off.

The airport was on the right. That much I remembered. I'd watched over my father's shoulder as planes appeared from behind the tall brush, their engines muffling the music on shore as they glided up. Sometimes people turned and watched, trying to guess what name was painted across each plane's side.

Air Jamaica?

No, the colors are all wrong.

Are you sure?

Yeah. Besides, Air Jamaica left twenty minutes ago.

After the engines faded, long after, I'd still hear the palm leaves fluttering, admitting surrender. Someone kicked me in the shin.

"Jesus!" I exclaimed, pain shooting up my leg.

"Watch your mouth!" the nun said.

"Easy," Barrett whispered. "Just tryin' to wake you up."

"Both of you, enough!" the nun said.

Barrett and I snapped forward. We were sitting on the cobblestone ground of the courtyard, fourth row from the nun who stood in front of us, lecturing on. She shifted her gaze to the other half of the class, so I let my body slump forward, closing my eyes. I wanted to feel the rush of my blue sea—but someone pinched me, Sara this time, keeping me in class.

"He died for all our sins," the nun said, "let Himself be

nailed to that cross to save us all." Behind her, the wooden cross creaked in the breeze, the timber black and rotting. "He died because He loved us," she said, "so much so that He made the ultimate sacrifice." Punched into the wood were hundreds of tiny holes, divots marring the grain. "Each one of these holes," she said, "is a mark of our sin and a sign of His love." She swiveled her gaze left, then right. "Can you imagine feeling a love that great?"

Smirking, I whispered to Sara, "So why can't I take Communion?"

"Shut up," Sara said.

"If I helped nail Him to the cross, and He died for me, then why can't I—"

"Shut *up*!" she hissed, leaning forward. "Think this is gonna be on the test?" Strands of her hair fell free from her ponytail, curling against her collar in ringlets of brown. She tucked her hair behind her ear then squinted. "Why are you staring at me?"

"You have moles."

"What?"

"Right here." I touched my finger to her skin. "Three little dots, *boop boop boop*." I let my finger linger in a soft caress. "It was one of the first things I noticed about you."

She leaned away. "What?"

My finger grew cold as her confusion turned to terror, then terror to disgust. What had I done? Sitting next to her, knees touching, feel the divide. It would be years before we'd both see it, let it bubble to the surface—but there it was, fiery and true, the churning desire to make Sara my girl.

Terrified and all mixed up, I stared at the ground, the grass, the cross, the dirty blond highlights on the back of someone's head. The nun, the cross, the door, the cross. The cross.

"What's with the cross, hmm?"

Sara blinked, still staring.

"They can't really expect us to believe those holes represent each and every one of our sins. I mean, seriously, think of how many billions of people there are, there's just no way—"

"What?"

"—that they could put all the sins of the whole wide world into one cross, that thing would be dust, I mean, if they're trying to be historically accurate—"

"Stop."

"What's going on back there?" the nun said.

"—in which case there were less people back then so maybe that'd be a little more feasible butIdon'tknowstillseemsfishyfish! likethecatholicsign!hahaha!"

"Slow down," Sara whispered. "I can't understand you when you go off with your accent like that."

"I don't have an accent," I sputtered, heart beating fast.

She raised her brow.

"I don't have an accent." I held my chest. "You do."

She blinked, blinked, let her brow fall. Hearing the heavy clack of shoes advancing, I looked up at the wrinkled face shrouded in black.

"Do you have something you would like to share with the class?" the nun said.

Your religion is boring and dumb. "No, miss."

"So what's all this chatter back here?" she said, her voice rising.

I turned to Sara then the nun, nothing to say. The nun stepped back, pointing to the door on the left. Stand up, accept punishment, same routine for the past two years. The nun led me through the doorway to detention as my classmates turned, they always turned, straining to see. Breathing deep, I closed my eyes and let myself escape inside.

I wondered how far out we were. The shelf was shallow, white sand peppered gray sprawling for miles. I'd strain to hear sounds from shore, Red Stripe clinking or spoons scraping against pots of rice and peas—anything to gauge how far away we were, like counting thunder. Sometimes my father would wander out until the cool water rushed up to my chest. Flailing against him, legs kicking, I'd feel his arms abandon my back.

"Exactly," he would say, "now let go."

But I wouldn't. I'd lock my arms and clench my eyes and I wouldn't let go. I'd hold on tighter, tighter. He'd sigh, carrying me farther out to sea.

I opened my eyes. Honey-scented candles lit the prayer room in Texas, wax melted low around thin flames. Detention, my chance to confess my sins before Christ. There, on the wall, just above eyeline—Jesus framed, his hand over his heart.

Outside, the bell rang. I heard doors bursting open, yelling and screaming invading my silence. A nun peered in. Eyes closed, pretend to repent: dear Catholic God, can you put Protestant God on the line? Apparently you two aren't the same thing, and you seem to think I'm doomed to hell. The nun stepped back, seeming satisfied, then walked away. I rocked side to side on the small cushion. What would they do if they saw me napping? Two columns of shadow streaked over my knees—Sara and Barrett staring in.

"Akua," Sara said, like *aqua*, too fast through the *u* and *a*.

"Akúa," I corrected her. She'd known me for two years and I still had to correct her.

"A-ku-a," she said again, slowly. "Ak*ua*, Akuuuuuaaaa," she said, trying to get it but falling short.

Barrett coughed.

Smiling, I whispered to him, "You still owe me five dollars. Don't think I've forgotten."

He laughed as lockers started slamming shut. Passing period was almost over. As the bell rang, Barrett turned and sprinted down the hall, but Sara lingered for a moment. From across the pool of light Sara looked at me, and waved.

Heat. Sweat. Loud whir of the struggling AC. Church service over, I come back to myself. Sitting in Tamika's car, I fill myself back up, flexing my fingers and wiggling my toes. I'm back home, but I still feel the need to dream. Tamika revs the engine then pulls out of the church lot.

We zoom down the straightaway, swerving left right left through the junction at Cross Roads. After the market, we pass a park lined with palm trees and neat lawns surrounding tall white structures gathered in the center.

"Statues? Art?" I ask Tamika.

"Tombstones," Tamika says. "That's National Heroes Park." I turn to the concrete tombstones stretching into the sky like hands despairing. A few minutes later, Tamika pulls into a small strip of concrete shacks, menus painted on old roofing hanging above each stall.

"For a treat," Tamika says.

I look at her. A treat?

A woman walks up as Tamika starts pointing to things on her menu. I have no idea what they're saying so I sit back, listening to the stiff peaks of consonants colliding against teeth. The woman says something, her vowels rolling deep, then waves to me. I nod, pretending to understand.

The woman goes back to her shack then returns with a round something wrapped in foil. She hands it to Tamika, who hands it to me, the lump still warm to the touch. I hold it close then sniff: roasted breadfruit. Tamika hands the woman a few bills then asks for something else. The woman beckons to someone in her shack.

"Bring tooartree widdal di sunting deh," the woman says.

Tamika relaxes into her seat while we wait.

Bring tooartree echoes through my head.

> twoartree
>
> *two* ar *three* widdal di
>
>> wid al di
>>
>> *with all* di

Bring two or three with all the— A teenage girl comes running, cradling three sweetsops against her chest. She says something to Tamika, offering them to her. Tamika pushes them away.

> *two or three with all the* sunting deh
>
>> *something* deh
>>
>> *something them*

Bring two or three with all the something them. The woman comes back, handing Tamika a steaming something wrapped in newspaper. I know what she said. Tamika gives the newspapered package to me. I heard the woman, knowing running through me thick and heady like roots in rich soil. Bring two or three sweetsops with the newspapered something them. Just show them the sweetsops, she was saying. Maybe they'll buy. Turning to my sister, I want to celebrate this small moment of coming home. But I can't. I don't. My tongue shrivels at the shame of admitting I was ever on the outside.

I open the newspaper and look inside. Steamed fish and breadfruit; *bush food*, Daddy would say. Down-home food. Breaking the breadfruit open with my thumbs, I give a chunk to Tamika then do the same with the fish.

"You were never baptized," Tamika says.

I keep chewing, breaking off more fish. What am I supposed to say? Tamika reaches for a bottle of water on the back seat. Her back turned, I crack the lip of Bryson's box and push a piece of breadfruit inside. A treat, brother. Tamika takes a swig of water then offers the bottle to me. I shake my head no. She breaks off more breadfruit then puts a chunk of fish on top.

"We should have Father Spencer baptize you while you're here," she says, popping the morsel into her mouth.

I let her sentence linger, clouding the car with the steam rising from our fish. She chews then swallows as her words float and fume. I take another bite then stare straight ahead. Taking a quick sip, she stops eating. She watches me. I chew my food then swallow. She moves her mouth like she might say it again, but stops. I wonder if her tongue's shriveled too—because there it is, naked and swirling. Get baptized. Join me. Join *me*. Be with me in this thing I know. There it is, her shy and desperate need.

"Sure," I finally respond.

She looks at me, gaze hopeful. "Is this another one of your jokes?"

I smile, offering her more breadfruit. My sister, dear sister. "No. Let's do it." A treat, for you.

SATURDAY

15 Days Left

TAMIKA PACKED ME A LUNCH, CORNED BEEF ON hard-dough bread with finger bananas for dessert. I told her I could just buy food on the road. She told me I was too loose with my money as she put the food in my bag. Careful on the number four bus, she said, it's always late and the driver will try to charge you more than the proper fare. And watch your wallet on King Street, nuff pickpocket dem a walk 'roun' in nice nice clothes. And always haggle with taxi drivers over the fare and agree on the price before you get in. And stick to the main streets, don't go walking down side roads you don't know. And if you get lost, say *Red Hills Road* and come home. And when your lunch is gone and your stomach is empty, come home. And when your feet grow tired, come home. And come home, come home. I hugged her, my nose against her collar, smelling peppermint.

Now Bryson and I are at the Arcade, browsing through rows of CDs and slanting racks of posters as a dancer spins on the stage outside. I'd forgotten this is what *Arcade* means here: not pinball or racing games or oily pizza on floppy paper plates, but clothes shops, record shops, restaurants facing each other in a rotunda around a stage beneath the open sky.

Moving to the back of the store, I pick up a pair of red pants then hold them against my waist. Too long. Besides, I don't need pants. I don't need anything but I came here and saw people moving, browsing, black like me, so I thought—me too. I shuffle out the doorway and toward another store. I've been here six days and there's still so much I haven't seen.

"Where should we go, brother?" I murmur, tapping the straps of my bag.

Onstage, the performer drops into a split, arms moving with the rhythm of the song. I stop to watch, feeling my stomach tighten and growl. Almost time for lunch.

"Are you following me?"

I turn around. The woman from the bus to Cross Roads— she's standing in front of me, headphones around her neck and music turned off.

"What?" I stammer.

"Mi will cut yuh, yuh nuh," she says, one hand on her hip and the other pointed at my face. I follow the line of her finger to her slender forearm and round face, wide-set eyes above sweet lips.

"What are you going on about?"

She kisses her teeth. "Yuh tink is joke mi a mek?"

I hold up my hands. "Listen, I'm not following you."

She wraps the straps of her handbag around her fist. "Yuh lie."

"I'm not lying." I step back. "Why would I lie? I don't—"

She takes a swing at me, her handbag grazing my cheek as I stumble backward into a man by the stage. He steadies me by the hips, holding me against him just long enough for me to feel his wallet, his keys, his dick hanging limp before he pushes me back into the fray. She takes another swing, the buckle hitting my arm.

"Is what yuh want?" she yells, rearing back for another swing.

"Rahtid," I exclaim. "Yuh jus' goi' box me down inna de street like so?"

She lets her arm fly as I reach out, her handbag whipping around my hand. I pull my fist toward my chest, yanking both her bag and her closer. She's breathing hard, standing just a few inches from me, still holding the other end. I can see dark freckles beneath the brown irises of her eyes.

"Woi!" the man exclaims then laughs.

She punches me in the chest, sending me backward. Smoothing her pants, she slings her bag over her arm. She looks harried. She looks pleased. Without a word, she pushes her way through the crowd as the dancer continues. I look around. I could leave the Arcade, eat my lunch somewhere far away from her. She walks into a jerk joint, making her way to a seat near the back.

"I'm not following you," I say again, standing in front of her. She takes off her headphones.

"I don't know why you think I am, but I'm not. I don't even know the roads well enough to follow you."

A server comes over, handing her a tray of jerk pork and festival.

"Who are you?" she says.

"Akúa."

She takes a bite of her pork.

"What's your name?" I ask her.

She leans close. "Are you strange?"

"What's your name?" I say again.

"Are you strange?" she insists.

I watch her, my tongue flooding with the need to roll her hard bulb against my teeth. "Yes," I murmur.

Relieved, she pushes the basket of food toward me. She ordered enough for two.

SUNDAY
14 Days Left

CLEAR WATER LAPS AGAINST BROWN SAND, WAVES glinting in the afternoon light. I look across the restaurant, hearing dominoes smacking against plastic tables and beer bottles clinking as Beenie Man rumbles on low.

"Dem neva cook dis one right," says the girl from Cross Roads. She breaks the snapper in half, handing me a piece.

"Why *lyme* and not lemon?" I take the food.

Her name is Jayda. After the Arcade, she invited me out to *lyme*—a new phrase for me, *lyme*. I thought it was something I'd forgotten after I left; turns out it's a new phrase that's taken root since.

Taking a bite, I gesture with the fish to the swaying trees and bustling restaurant and the beer bottles cluttering the small table between her and me. "Doesn't it seem strange to use the name of a sour fruit for such a sweet enterprise?"

To lyme: to meet up and hang out somewhere around town, maybe with bottles of Red Stripe, maybe with baskets of bammy and fried fish. That morning, over breakfast, Tamika asked where I planned on going today. *To lyme with a girl*, I wanted to say then I remembered Tamika's fist on my face so I lied and said I was going to see the Giddy House at Port Royal.

"Lawd have mercy," Jayda says. "*Why use a sour fruit for such a sweet enterprise?* Where yuh from?"

"Here." I swallow my food. "Kingston. You?"

"Yuh from here an' yuh talk like dat?" She laughs. "Cyaa be Kingston yuh come from."

I lean forward. "How exactly am I supposed to sound, if I'm truly from here?"

She breaks off a piece of bammy then stuffs it in my mouth. "Yuh suppose fi talk like yuh have sense." She lets her hand linger, forefinger and thumb pressed against my tongue. She's funny. She's mean. I close my mouth around her fingers as she pulls away.

Two tables over, a beer bottle shatters, sending waves of frothy yellow across the concrete floor. A woman wearing a bright pink wig leans down, napkins in hand and bangs falling across her eyes. She glances at Jayda then me.

"So, Akúa," Jayda says, "gyal who talk like she come from foreign but seh she bawn jus' yah so, what brings you to beautiful Jamaica?"

"My brother." I take another bite of bammy.

"Where him live?" she says.

"He's dead."

"You came back for the funeral?"

"I am the funeral." I crush a small rock beneath my heel.

Smoke wafts from the open-air kitchen behind us, low clouds carrying the smell of curry conch and simmering fish tea. I take a swig of my beer.

"What do you do for work?" I ask Jayda.

She hands me another piece of fish as the woman in the pink wig passes our table, a fresh plate of food in hand. Jayda smiles at her as she squeezes past.

"I was in school for criminology. Mi graduate two years ago," Jayda says. "I applied for a job with the police. They come tell me they reach their quota of females for the foreseeable future."

I cringe. Quota of *females*? "Is that really what they called you?" I take another swig. "*Females?* Not even women, *females?*"

She chuckles. "Is that really all it takes to offend you?"

The woman in the wig sits down, gathering her skirt between her knees as she starts to eat. She's too skinny. She has no chest. And she needs to shave, dark shadow of stubble along her jawline and chin. But she's watching us.

"Who is that woman?" I whisper to Jayda.

Jayda looks at me, surprised. "You know that's a woman?"

"Well, yeah, what?" The slight sashay of her hips as she walked by told me she's a woman. "Why is she staring at us?"

Jayda moves her leg so it's touching mine then blows the woman a kiss.

MONDAY

13 Days Left

"To wha?" Daddy says.

"To lyme," I say again, switching the phone to my left ear.

It's just after breakfast, heat blowing in through the open window. Tamika went back to work today, but I can smell nutmeg and condensed milk wafting from the cornmeal porridge cooling on the stove. *Mek sure yuh eat*, Tamika said as she left, pointing to the bowls, the bread, the butter to put on the toast. I laughed then told her yes, I'm not two, I understand, and she pulled me in for a hug. My nose in her shirt, I smelled peppermint again but this time, just beneath it, there was something entirely her own. I closed my eyes and breathed deep. Sorrel. Tart sweetness of sorrel, fragrant and freshly dried.

"What dat mean, *lyme*?" Daddy says.

"To hang out."

"So yuh hang out 'pon wah lime?"

Laughing, I stretch out across the living room couch. "No,

Daddy. She wants to hang out, and the phrase for hanging out is, 'Let's link up and lyme.'"

The woman in the wig was Jayda's friend. Jayda asked her to come and keep watch in case I turned out to be mad mad *mad*.

"Oh," he says. "Is new ting dat?"

"So they say."

"*Lyme*," he says then chuckles. "Mi backside."

Sitting up, I reach for my mug on the coffee table and take a long sip.

"Akúa," my father says, his voice low and misting like settling dew, "how are you?"

I remember now, I remember why I called. My father is a rough man, as soft and nurturing as craggy earth. But he is solid. He is present. I hear his voice and feel the sure firmness beneath my feet. "I'm okay, Daddy."

"Good," he says. "Sara sent you mail."

My hand slips, sending black tea pooling around the edges of Bryson's box.

"Want me to open it?" he says.

Groaning, I get up to grab a rag from the kitchen. "Sure."

Sounds of ripping paper fills the phone. Daddy grunts.

"What does it say?"

"It's instructions on how to wire her money," he says. "Damage deposit from your apartment, I think."

"Is that all?" I've known Sara for ten years, as long as I've been away from home, and all she wants to talk about is money? I watch my spilled tea drip off the table and pool on the floor. "Daddy, is that all Sara's letter says?"

He hesitates. "Yes."

"You sure?"

"Yup."

"Daddy." Rag in hand, I walk back to the coffee table. "Never in my twenty years have I ever heard you say *yup*." I've heard *yes*, I've heard *yea, man*, I've heard *sure*, but never *yup* like Barrett or Sara or even me after years and years of living abroad. He's trying to be easy. He's lying to me.

"Akúa," he says, "ease up deh likkle. A nuh lack a tongue mek cow nah talk." He's trying to spare me but I want to know. It's my mail, I deserve to know.

"What does it—"

"No," Daddy says.

"But—"

"No."

Does she miss me? Does she blame me? Dropping the rag on the coffee table, I watch the cloth turn from white to brown. "Sounds weird when you say it."

"Wha?" he says.

"*Yup*." I move the rag around to soak up the spilled tea. "Sounds weird and wrong when you say it."

He chuckles. "How mi mus' say it den?"

I move my lips to form the word then stop, hearing something scuttle on my left.

"Where's your sister?" Daddy says.

"At work."

Scuttle-scuttle behind the couch.

"How much longa yuh a stay?" he says.

"Jus' a likkle while longer." I bought my ticket on a flash sale then told him I'd wait to buy the return to see if I'd get just as lucky. "Daddy, what else does the letter say?"

He goes quiet, just the sound of his breathing filling the receiver.

"It's my mail!" I exclaim. "You can't keep me from knowing what's in my mail. I'm pretty sure that's a federal crime or something."

He chuckles.

"Daddy!"

He laughs outright.

Annoyed, I throw the rag over the bar and watch it land in the sink. "Well, I'm glad at least one of us is amused."

"Tek care of yuhself," Daddy says, still chuckling.

"Yeah yeah," I respond as he hangs up.

I put the phone back on its hook. Standing in the quiet, I hear a soft *scuttle* on my right. Sara sent me mail. *Scuttle-scuttle* a cockroach darts between my feet, rushing toward the kitchen door. Lurching forward, I grab the first hard thing I can then bring it down in a wet thud. Maybe she wrote to say she hates me. Or maybe she wants me back but can't find me. The thud echoes off the walls as I look at what I've done. The top of Bryson's box shines, smooth and glossy in the fluorescent light. Picking him up, I scrape the cockroach off his bottom and into the trash. This is good. It is dead. But I still ache.

TUESDAY

12 Days Left

OUR FORKS AND KNIVES CLANG AGAINST OUR plates as my sister smiles at me across her kitchen table. She's made brown stew chicken and boiled banana, fried plantain and callaloo for dinner. This is the biggest meal we've had together.

I tried to help her cook all this. I made a move toward the knife so I could chop the garlic, the onions, anything, but she grabbed my arm and told me no. "You're the guest of honor!" she said. "I'm not a guest," I told her, "I've come home." She gave me a soft smile like I'd said something adorable then told me dinner would be ready in jus' a likkle bit. I sat in the living room and watched her work, smells intensifying in the small apartment. Sara sent me mail. Four years my Sara, and all she wants is cash.

"I spoke to Father Spencer today," Tamika says as we sit down to eat. "He's agreed to baptize you during next week's service." She serves herself a heaping of callaloo. "He might also welcome others from the congregation to step forward too. Not sure."

I watch her over the steaming bowls as she chews her food, sighing in silent contemplation. She means to do good for the safety of my soul. I shove piece after piece of plantain in my mouth to keep from screaming, *No*. This is a treat, for her.

After dinner, I thank her for the delicious food. She takes my empty plate then says, "Let us give thanks for the goodness these hands have made," and I say, "Yes." I don't know what she means, but *yes*. She sits us down on the couch and clasps my hands in hers, bowing her head to pray. Staring at my shoes, I listen to her fervent whisper and wish I could join her, be together with her in swimming with belief.

Later, with the plates washed and leftovers put away, I make my way down the hall to sit cross-legged on my bed and stare at my brother's box. "Hey," I murmur. In the room next to mine, I hear the soft click of Tamika turning off her bedside lamp. "I've missed you," I murmur, my voice disappearing into the sheets, the rug. "I've missed—I, I miss you."

"Sara and I broke up," I whisper. "We'd been fighting for months. I thought maybe, if we talked it out, I don't know." The vape mat crackles in the corner, thin smoke swirling around my suitcase and shoes. "Sara wanted me to move with her to some state I've never been to for med school, but I couldn't—I can't. I just don't have it in me to start all over again." I rub the sheets, hearing the zap of a mosquito meeting its hot end. "I did the right thing, right?" I ask.

Of a box. I'm talking to a box. But this box is Bryson, who spat up on me as a baby in Jamaica and stole my taquitos in Texas then pushed me into the snow in Canada. Bryson, who was there through all the moves, annoying or ignoring or imploring me to always come back to him. I kneel in the presence of my brother and feel at home. I want him to feel like he's with me too.

"Tamika!" I bang on the wall separating our rooms. "You awake?"

"Lawd God," she says. "I am now."

"Tomorrow!" I yell. "Let's go to the beach!"

Muffled sounds of sheets ruffling and feet thudding echo through the cinder block wall. Tamika flings open the door to my room.

"Pickni, is wha—" My pillow thumps against her hip. I grab my other pillow, ready to throw.

"Beach!"

Tamika picks up the pillow. "Ak—"

I throw my other pillow and miss, watching it bounce off the doorframe and onto the floor.

Tamika looks down at me sitting cross-legged on the small bed.

"Beach? Please?"

She throws both pillows and hits me in the head. "As you wish, Your Highness."

WEDNESDAY

11 Days Left

"**H**ELLSHIRE," TAMIKA SAYS AS WE DRIVE THROUGH the gate and onto the long stretch of white sand. She called in sick to work, faking coughs into the gray receiver. I could hear her boss berating her, telling her not to make a habit of neglecting her duties, especially so soon after taking vacation. Tamika rolled her eyes and croaked, *Of course.*

We park behind a row of cement shacks, exhaust rising from some of their zinc roofs. From somewhere down the beach, I hear dancehall booming. Stopping at one of the shacks, I buy a plate of steam bammy and escovitch fish from a man with dreadlocks tied down beneath an old shirt. Tamika tries to order for me, squaring up to him with her brow creased and scowl ready. I pretend I have no idea who she is. He laughs and slaps my back. I order for myself and probably pay too much, only understanding *okra* and *kingfish* as the rasta stirs the simmering sauce. But I'm trying, I tell myself. I'm here too and I am trying.

Tamika orders after me, her face still in a scowl and voice deadpan. I look up at the sky, expecting to see planes swooping close. Food in hand, we walk across the hot sand to find a place to eat. Tamika sits first, putting her shoes beside her and pulling her skirt around her knees. I stay standing, listening to the *boomboom* of dancehall thumping, until Tamika grabs my elbow and drags me down.

We sit and we eat as I look all around at women moving slowly through the crowd, selling cotton candy and CheezTrix from packages clipped to wire hangers. Breaking the skin of my fish, I watch little girls dancing near the shore, their hands on their knees and backs arched in the air as they move like the grown-ups daggering in the waves. I bite into the bammy and stuff some fish in my mouth as wah fu-fool bwoy come rub up on wah 'ooman and nearly knock de gyal inna de sea and I rip more fish off the bone as a woman sets up shop under a palm tree, laying out tie-dye T-shirts and beach towels painted with sunsets for sale. I watch a father putting floaties on his son as I bite into more bammy and a toddler waddles past, an open diaper wedged between her butt cheeks as I chew and swallow and reach for "Slow down" more fish, sauce dripping down my fingers and into the hot sand. And I watch teenagers strolling in the surf and *boomboomboom* from speakers "Slow down!" Tamika says, "You're going to make yourself sick," and I eat and I eat with eyes and mouth feeling so warm and full I could puke.

I take the keys and waddle back to the car, leaving Tamika behind. I lift Bryson from the passenger floor, fumbling with the box. There's a cove somewhere around here. I remember scrambling over sandy rock behind Daddy's strong legs as he led us up, up, toward a wooden stairway winding through thick brush then down, down, to the small shore. Does Tamika remember it too? I gesture for her to join. She sees the box then gives me that stare, that white-as-ghost stare, and stays where she is. Sighing, I leave her behind. Weaving through the food shacks, I find the stairway leading up and over the rocks.

Overhead the trees rustle and sway, leaves overhanging in a dense green shroud against clear sky. Holding my flip-flops, I slide my foot along each stair, my toes digging into the packed-tight earth shored up by wood. Bare feet against hard ground, I feel the ridges in each stair, deep and etched like rivulets dividing; skin against earth, so much easier to sense, to know. Bryson and I continue down, down, feeling through the brush toward the crashing waves.

In the cove the noise quiets a bit, only a few children poking at crabs scuttling between their feet. I find a spot, a nice flat spot between two boulders where the sand ripples with the shape of the sea. Mixing a bit of him with the wet sand, I make a castle—small but fancy, the kind of castle that would've made my Bryson proud. I lean back to look at my work and notice a young boy watching me. He's going to smash the castle as soon as I leave. Might as well. If not him, then the waves.

Standing up, I snap the box of my brother's ashes shut as heat bathes the back of my neck. *Feel good, eee?* Daddy would say. And it does, so I turn my head toward the sun.

THURSDAY

10 Days Left

SMELLS OF CARAMELIZED ONION AND COCO-
nut milk hang in heavy clouds above bubbling pots.
We're in the apartment. Tamika's making dinner, but
this time she's letting me help. I stir the stew peas then turn the
rice off.

"Bwoy mi a tell yuh," Tamika says as she wipes down the dining table, "mi naa look forward fi go a work tomorrow mawnin'."

"Why?" I ask her.

She turns on the radio then grabs two plates. "I have a new
manager," she says. "I don't think she and I are going to get
along." The newscaster's voice comes in and out of focus, teasing
tidbits of the stories to come. "Mi ask har, mi manager, I ask
her when she needs me to complete the review of the accounts
she gave me. She says end of day will be *quite all right*. Can yuh
believe dat? *Quite all right* like she a have tea wid the Queen. Mi
backside!" Tamika laughs, putting the plates then the cutlery in
front of our two seats.

Checking the plantain, I give the rice a quick fluff. "Tamika?"

"Hmm?"

"Where do you work?"

"Oh!" she exclaims with a nervous laugh. We talked on the phone most Sundays for years, and I don't know where she works.

"Jamaica Power Service," she says, walking over to me then taking the plantain out of the oil. *Chiffon, a family affair*, the radio echoes, going to commercial.

"Doing what?"

"Accounts specialist," Tamika says, lining the plantain up on a piece of paper towel.

"Since when?"

"A few years." Turning off the burners, she carries the rice and stew peas to the table.

"How many years?"

Tamika grabs the plantain, setting it down by the rice.

"Was that your first job?" I lean forward. "After UWI, I mean. Did you go straight there or did you work somewhere else first?" Tell me stories like you used to. Tell me everything. "Do you like it?" I ask her. "How big is your team?" I rest my chin in my hands, my palms tingling with heat remembered from Sunday after Sunday of cradling the phone close.

"Is this what they teach you abroad?" Tamika says. "To heal up everything with nice-nice talk?"

The broadcast comes back, a little ditty bouncing through the speakers to announce the start of the evening news.

"Let us pray," Tamika says.

She bows her head but I don't join her. I just listen to her words mumbled hot and fast.

"Anyway," she says, reaching for the rice, "is *quite all right* but me and her will work it out. She's a manager. That's how she's supposed to talk."

She puts two scoops of rice on my plate. So that's it? Exhaling hard, I let the moment pass. I will get no answers, so I force a chuckle. "So she's supposed to talk like she's British royalty? Who still believes in that shit?" I stab two pieces of plantain and put them on my plate.

Tamika watches me eat, forehead creased in deep thought as the news begins. Two-car pileup on the road leading to Spanish Town. Both drivers in critical condition. Tamika puts down her fork. She picks it back up. She puts it down then leans across the table toward me.

"If you ask me," Tamika says, "we never should have left the Crown."

"What?"

All traffic closed in both directions. Motorists advised to avoid.

"Under the British," Tamika says, "our government made sense."

"What?" I put down my knife. "What are you talking about? How did we get here?"

Tamika pops a piece of stew beef into her mouth then looks at me, shoulders back and chest proud. She's looking for a fight.

"Are you serious right now?" I lean forward. "They enslaved the Arawaks then worked them to the point of near extinction.

They packed us in ships and shackled us to this island that we had never heard of or wanted to see. To willingly re-submit to that kind of system, where everything's designed to make sure we lose—"

"So that's it, then?" Tamika says. "It's all that simple? The Brits were bad, we were good, and we should all go back to Africa?"

The newscaster clears her throat. The Jamaican dollar continues to fall, thirty-five JMD to one USD.

Tamika stabs at her stew peas. "More people ate under the British. More people had clean wata." She licks a bit of sauce off her thumb.

"More people died under the British—"

"Yuh tink dem not deddin' now?"

Foreign investors expected to arrive in the coming days. Minister of Finance hopeful for lessening Jamaica's dependence on the International Monetary Fund.

"Listen to this shit," Tamika says. *"Minista o' Finance?* Who de backside tell us we need someone name a minister to look over our finances? Is who government dis if we a jus' play Big Man inna smaddy else pantomime?"

Three dead in an armed robbery in downtown Kingston. One other in critical condition—a child.

"Dem shackle us to de lan' and to dem systems and now we a do it to we own self. Plenty minista a tek bribe an' let foreign investa come do whateva dem dyam please, den turn 'roun' an' seh we need IMF 'cause de money dry up." Tamika shovels rice

onto her fork then tries to pile peas on top. The food falls off as
the news prattles on.

Doctors are hopeful the child will live. Members of the com-
munity are asked to step forward with any pertinent information.
The police have no leads.

"Yuh want yuh storytime?" she says. "Well, here it is. Nice-
nice jus' fi yuh, welcome home." I watch her as she chews. "It was
a white government run by white people," Tamika says. "Our
government made sense."

"That's not—" My appetite goes cold. "There has to be something better."

Tamika laughs. "I'm all ears, Akúa." She serves herself more
rice. "The whole country is all ears."

After dinner, I stack the plates in the sink then put the pots
to soak. Tamika's still talking but I'm not listening. I bag up
the trash and put the leftovers in the fridge. I spray down the
counters and put out a fresh roach trap. After a while, she stops
talking. I grab the sponge and start wiping down the stove.
She looks me over with a threatening *hmm* then retreats to her
room.

My sister once knew how to be soft, feeding me stories like
pap to the infirm. She knew how to comfort me, how to make
me feel whole. There was the time I called and told her we were
moving—"again," I sobbed, "we're moving *again*." Kingston to
Texas and then Texas to Canada—and she listened to me, she
heard me then. She stayed on the phone and fed me stories of
home to soothe my grief.

"Daddy says we're moving," I remember telling her as snot dribbled down my chin.

"I know," she said. "He called."

I looked around the emptying house in Texas, our clothes and shoes all packed up *again*.

When I asked Daddy why, he said everything there in Texas cost too much. "Ova charge an' ova charge den come chat 'bout acktivity fee?" he said. "Cho!" They need money for school fee then money for uniforms then money for new books then for class trips then for school plays and for little pumpkins they send home with carving kits then "come talk 'bout mi mus' dress up mi pickney dem like duppy fi some fu-fool Halloween. Is what kinda foolishness dat?" Daddy had said then kissed his teeth.

Daddy told me all this at three in the afternoon on a school day, I told Tamika, and he was still in his pajamas. Three in the afternoon and Daddy was walking around the kitchen barefoot and unshowered, steam rising from the mug in his hand. That's when I realized—earlier that morning, when Bryson and I rode to school with Barrett because we thought Daddy was gone, maybe he wasn't. Maybe he was in his room, in his bed, the sheets pulled over his head. My sister, dear sister, I think our father had lost his job. Which meant he lost his visa. Which meant me and my brother, we'd lost our visas too. After all the money spent to send us to a private Catholic school, there was nothing left to buy us time, to keep us safe. *Then why*, I wanted to yell, *why did you send us to such an expensive school?*

"How yuh mean?" Tamika said through the phone.

I wiped my runny nose.

"How yuh mean, *expensive school?*" she said.

I told Tamika there was more than the Catholic school, that there was somewhere else Bryson and I could've been. I told her I knew because of the girls I met once at a playground, black girls with elbows greased and baby hairs laid as their ropes flew dizzy one inside the other, closing in on their place of whistle and song.

My father had driven me to a park in a faraway part of town. I didn't want to go. I wanted to stay home and press play and see Miss Lou's eyes so round and fiery with all the heat of home. But Daddy dragged me from my room then drove me to the park—a long strip of lawn between two brick buildings, asphalt road beyond.

All around me were black boys with rattails swinging and black girls sitting in stockings rife with runs. No one looked at me funny there, no one stared, everyone running and screaming in quick blurs—black, black, dark like me. Smiling, I spread my arms and I rushed forward, ready for them to scoop me up and pull me in. Two girls were setting up for jump rope on the edge of the lawn.

"Can I join?" I asked them.

The girl nearest looked at me, long braids swinging around her face. "Whatchu say?"

"I want to play." I grinned at her. "Is that all right?" Shaking out my legs, I started warming up to skip.

Another girl came closer, the bun on her head round and taut like the pooch of her stomach. "What'd she say?" she said to her friend.

Her friend shrugged as they both looked at me, waiting. They didn't understand—so I cleared my throat and flattened my tongue into the language I'd been taught would be understood everywhere.

"May I join?" I asked in proper English, the Queen's English. "I'd like to be part of your game."

The one with the braids burst out laughing. "Quit playin'," she said.

"I'm serious," I told her, stepping closer. "I'd really love to join."

They both laughed, the girl with the bun slapping my arm. "Where you from?" she said. "You sound like a dang Oreo."

A what?

"Comin' up in here wit' yo Oreo-lookin' ass," the girl with the braids said.

They laughed harder, squeezing my arms like I was supposed to laugh along too. I wanted to play, so I picked up a rope to show them what I meant. With my feet together, I swung the rope over my head in a simple round-and-round.

The girl with the bun stopped me. "We doin' double dutch," she said. "This ain't gym class."

"What's a double dutch?" I'd never heard of it. They must have made it up. "Did you make it up?"

She snickered. "You funny," she said. "I ain't never heard nobody talk like you."

"Double dutch," the one with the braids said. "Don't you know?"

"Yeah, girl," said her friend. "Don't you?"

I didn't. So, laughing, they pushed me out of the way and handed off the ropes to two of their friends who started swinging them through the air in quick *thwack-thwacks*. The two girls jumped in. Their friends alternated the ropes, one inside the other, one inside the other, like two whisks of a mixer with the girls caught in the middle. The girls jumped *left right left spin-round left right left* as the ropes flew faster, faster. They started singing a song. All four knew the words, singing as they skipped, and a crowd gathered around. *Left right left* they crossed their feet! I couldn't believe it but they crossed their feet, landing graceful with the rope between their legs before jumping right back up and doing a double hop. The whole crowd started singing as the girls spun around, crossed their feet, then added in claps as they jumped *left right left*. This was beautiful.

"Double dutch," I murmured as the crowd thickened, pressing in. Old faces, young faces, aunties holding babies, and boys dribbling basketballs all stopped to watch, their bodies moving to the *thwack thwack* of this beauty. My body was still, out of time with theirs. I didn't know what this game meant and I didn't know how to ask. What if this nice boy next to me called me an Oreo too? I didn't know what that was, but the girls' sick laughter told me it was not a thing I should want to be. So I slipped away. No one noticed me leave, the throng closing up to fill my cold space.

Standing at the edge of the playground, I started to cry. I wanted to play netball. Did they know netball? I knew netball. I wanted to be back on the court, jersey damp with sweat and licking glucose from my hand. I wanted to compete for my house on sports day. I wanted to scream, *Go, Red House, go!* then watch the girls from my form line up for the sprint. I wanted to be back in the blender of things I knew.

"That's where I should have been," I told Tamika. She sighed on the other end of the phone. I should have been at school with them. But their shoes were worn and shirts starting to fade. When we got in our car to drive home, I saw them sitting on the sidewalk waiting for the city bus. I looked at my father and knew, no matter the cost, I never would have gone to their school. The busted doors and flustered teachers and crowded classrooms we saw on TV in Jamaica—my father would have scraped his pockets bare before sending me and my brother to those schools. That's why we'd left Jamaica, to avoid the aching anger of never enough.

"What should I do?" I asked Tamika. "How should I—" I couldn't stop crying.

"Remember the patty place next to Daddy's barber?" Tamika said.

"What?"

"Dem knock it down," she said. "Yuh rememba?"

I did remember. When I was a kid, while Daddy sat in the black chair with the clippers buzzing over his head, I'd sneak over to the patty shop and spend my allowance on coco bread so hot and fresh it would singe the roof of my mouth. "Tamika, we're moving."

"Just listen to me," she said. She started telling me that they ripped the building down to build some store called Price Is Smart, a big sign on top of the rubble screaming COMING SOON. "Whole heap o' new store, dem," she said, describing signs for a soon-to-be furniture store and a clothing store, maybe even a jerk grill.

I stopped crying as I listened, closing my eyes to imagine myself testing the knobs on a new washing machine or running my hand over a velvet sofa with a matching settee. She talked about renovations to the downtown bus depot, so I imagined fresh asphalt, white lines, clean walls "an' wah shopping center," she said, so I switched to bright lights and polished floors and "new playground for di school down de street," so slides, swings, brown and gray with plastic seats and "new highway," and she was losing me, I tried to concentrate and stay with her to see what she saw, but she was pulling away into a future as close as a cloud, as real as the monsters I saw in my dreams. I opened my eyes, the top of my mouth hot with mourning.

"Akúa," Tamika said, "yuh hearin' me? It's Mummy's birthday today."

"It is?"

"Yes," she said. "How could you forget?"

I rubbed my hand over my hair. I remembered we used to eat black cake on her birthday—each bite moist and fruity, fingers wet with port. "Maybe you could buy her a gift from one of those new stores," I quipped.

Tamika didn't laugh. I cleared my throat, remembering the ditty about birthdays we used to watch with Miss Lou.

"*Happy birthday,*" I croaked, "*happy birthday, happy birthday to you, dear Mummy, happy birthday.*"

"Stop," Tamika said. "Why yuh a use proppa voice? It ruin de tune." She coughed then cleared her throat too. " *'Appy birt'day,*" she sang, "'*appy birt'day, 'appy birt'day to yuh, dear Mummy, 'appy birt'day!*"

"*Now, dis is de birt'day song fah Mummy from everyone,*" I joined in. "*Enjoy yuh special day, now, Mummy, mek sure yuh 'ave some fun! 'Appy birt'day.*"

Tamika started clapping her hand against her chest as we sang together. "*'Appy birt'day, 'appy birt'day to yuh now, Mummy, 'appy birt'day!*"

We both laughed, our voices rolling like the audience's in the tapes. I loved Miss Lou's birthday song. Sometimes I'd make Mummy sing it to me, just because.

"Clap yuhself," Tamika said, and I wasn't crying anymore. I was singing a song I used to know with my sister who was in the place she'd always been. "Nuh worry yuhself wid *move here* or *move dere*. You know where you come from," Tamika said, and I sighed. "But bwoy, mi a tell yuh, mi nuh undastan' how they have the money to build all these shopping centers but dem still cyaa fix all de dyam pothole dem." And back then, on the phone, I laughed.

But now that I'm home, Tamika has no more stories to tell. Dinner over, she's fast asleep down the hall, snores echoing from around her shut door. I sweep the kitchen floor. I straighten our shoes. I sit on the couch in the dark. The tree frogs keep chirping and a dog starts barking and an orange light recedes to nothing as a car zooms past, headlights bouncing off the bare walls. Me, just me. I grab the phone from its hook, cord uncurling in soft snaps.

"Come man," Jayda says, giving me the address of a club and telling me what time we'll meet. "Tomorrow," she says, "come."

FRIDAY

9 Days Left

IT'S 10:00 P.M. THE CLUB REEKS OF SWEET excess. There's a stage, a red-lit stage, lights shining on then off, on then off over gold-painted walls and poles shining silver. I squeeze my way through the crowd, music booming through the feral haze of bodies pressed close. Shoulders tense, I suck my stomach in to make myself smaller, closing myself in against the crowd toasting and whining to the beat. This club is more raucous, more unruly than anywhere I've ever been. Arms pressed into my sides, I *sorry* and *'xcuse* my way through the pulsing throng. I walk up a set of spiral stairs near the back, neon signs for J.B.'s and Appleton lighting the way to the upstairs balcony. I edge my way past couples clogging the concrete walkway with their dancing. A barman walks through a set of double doors at the other end of the balcony and leaves the door ajar, revealing another room with couches, stools, a disco ball spinning slow, and a hallway beyond. I find a seat next to the bar, where Jayda told me to wait.

"Yuh naa drink?" the barman says as he leans forward, looking at me with two lazy eyes. He's shorter than me, skinny, a long scar down his arm.

"Jus' some wata," I stammer.

"Yuh a wait pon fren?" he says, scooping ice into a plastic cup.

I push my hands in my pockets, rummaging for change. He shakes his head no.

"Wait pon yuh fren dem," he says, handing the cup with ice water to me then bumps his fist against mine. Exhaling in relief, I take a sip then settle back onto my stool.

"'Ay, gyal!" Jayda walks through the double doors, an outfit draped over her arm. "How yuh do?" She waves at the barman then cotches on the stool next to mine. "What are you drinking?" she says. She looks languid. She looks easy. I take a deep breath and force my shoulders down.

"Vodka."

The barman laughs.

"Big 'ooman," Jayda says, getting up to lead the way through the double doors.

I wait a moment, letting her get a few steps ahead. She flips her hair over her shoulder in a gentle *come here*. I can tell she's used to leading the way.

"She's with me," Jayda says to the guard leaning against the wall. He nods but keeps watching me, his sneer never leaving.

We pass a staircase on our right and locked rooms on our left as Jayda opens another door at the end of the hall—and I follow. Watching her hips, I forget about my sister and follow a back of her, obedient and good. Inside the small room women bustle past, curlers in their hair and bras undone as the smells of nail polish and lotion swirl around my head.

"What is this?"

"Where I work," Jayda says.

A woman hobbles past me, wearing mesh panties and only one heel as she coats her legs in baby oil. Jayda watches me piece it together, her smirk spreading into a grin. This is a strip club. Jayda's a stripper. She takes off her shoes then pats my cheek.

"Have a refill," she says, pointing to a table of half-empty bottles.

I flatten myself against the wall to keep from getting bowled over as three women rush in, their pants already undone and shirts halfway over their heads. This is a strip club. My heart pounds in my chest. *This is a strip club.* Uncapping the rum, I give myself a generous pour.

"Kuyah!" a woman yells. "How yuh jus' come up in here and a jus' start drink? Fasty like wha!"

"I, uh—" I look around for Jayda.

"Yuh see dis?" the woman says, nudging someone beside her. "Gyal nuh 'ave no broughtupsy."

"Fi true fi true," the other woman says. "She jus' start drink like snake from desert."

I make to put down the drink, but I watch the happy shake of their stomachs and smiles passed like secrets and stop. I think they're jiving me.

Kissing my teeth, I press the bottle straight to my lips. "Mi nuh have no time fi yuh boderation."

Everyone laughs, the woman closest slapping me on the

back. I'm in. I got the joke. My heart's still pounding. I take a long glug of rum. Jayda comes out from behind a screen stripped down to her underwear and bra.

"Unnu start in five," a man yells through the door.

Jayda slips on her heels then hands me a spray bottle.

"What's this?" I ask her.

She turns around then spreads her legs, back arched so her thong catches the edge of the light. She looks back at me and waits. Shaking the bottle, I spray baby oil over her shoulders, her neck, then down the soft dip of her spine. I cover her thighs, my free hand following the spray up and over her calves to hips protruding like surprises from her small waist. I spray the backs of her arms then wipe it off and spray her again.

"Too much," someone says.

A woman hands Jayda a towel then Jayda hands the towel to me. I clean up my mess, wiping her hips and legs in deep strokes, heat pulsing from chest to arm to hand.

"Stay," Jayda says, taking her place in line.

"Of course," I respond, watching her leave.

Alone in the dressing room, I take another swig of rum. I've never been to a strip club before. For a few seconds as the booze warms my throat, I wonder if Tamika's ever been to one either. The door opens, bodyguard coming in to stare me down.

"I'm going, I'm going," I tell him, slipping out the room.

Walking down the hallway, I feel a cool draft to my left. Someone's standing at the bottom of the stairs, leaning into the alley to catch the evening breeze.

"Nuh bodda let in de vermin," the bodyguard says, gesturing to the person by the stairs.

"Yuh see me a bodda yuh?" the person says. It's a woman, broad shoulders and pink hair swooped to one side. It's Jayda's friend, the woman from the jerk pit.

"I don't do women," she says, noticing me staring.

"Who are you?"

She leans into the hall. "Madonna," she says.

"Like the singer or the saint?"

She smiles. "Both." Behind her, I hear feet thudding against pavement. Madonna slips out.

"Tek care, honey," she says as the door swings shut.

Madonna, I mouth to myself, making my way through the double doors and back to the dance floor. The club's grown louder, the mass of us smalling up ourselves, making space within the hot compress of night. Jayda's onstage, her ass to the crowd and pole between her breasts. She's starting to sweat, fat beads on thin oil. The people in the crowd, they grind as she twirls and I drink.

Leaning against the bar for a rest, I feel something cold slip into my hand. The barman laughs, eyes swinging to my left. Sipping the water, I stumble toward the dressing room.

"Marcus!" It's Madonna. "Marcus, pour me wah drink nuh?" She's at the top of the stairs that lead to the alley, gazing into the club.

The barman scoops and serves, scoops and serves, his eyes never swinging to her.

"Marcus!" Madonna yells. "Yuh hearin' me?"

"Mi naa serve no batty bwoy," he says.

The bodyguard huffs toward Madonna, raising his hand. Closing her eyes, she waits. The bodyguard's hand hangs open, waiting, like collecting rent. She pulls a wad from her bra and gives him half.

"Seh tanks," he says as he counts the bills.

She kisses her teeth then disappears down the stairs. Stumbling into the dressing room, I nearly trip over a woman by a suitcase.

"Who dis?" she says.

"Jayda's gyal," someone whispers.

"Jayda's *gyal*? Lawd Jesus," the other responds as I slump against the wall. "Mi always did wonda—"

"Cool yuhself nuh man," her friend says. "Look pon har, she somebody likkle baby fi true."

Grabbing me by the shoulders, she leads me to a chair. I close my eyes and wait for the room to settle. Jaw slack, I fall asleep.

Everything's quieter now, walls vibrating to the bass of something slow. My neck aches. I don't know how long I've been asleep. Opening the door, I hear glass cracking underfoot and a *slapslap* to my left. The hallway light's broken, filament scattered down the stairs leading to the alley. *Slapslap*, it's Marcus. He's fucking. He grabs at her skin as the woman claws at the stairs. He's pulled her shirt up over her head, pulled it tight like a hood. I can't see her face. I don't know if she's enjoying it.

"Is what yuh a look pon?" he yells with a grin.

He keeps going, keeps fucking her, his eyes pointed to my left. Jayda grabs my shirt, gesturing with her chin for me to go.

SATURDAY

8 Days Left

TAMIKA SHAKES ME AWAKE. "WHERE WERE YOU last night?"

Last night. The club. Opening my mouth, I feel my dry lips cracking, corners starting to bleed.

"Come on," Tamika says, walking to the door. There are two VHS tapes chucked under her arm. "I know it's not Sunday, but I figured." She smiles then shrugs. She wants to hang out, to *lyme*.

I close my eyes. "I went to a strip club last night."

"Strip club?" she says, voice dripping with disgust.

I nod.

"Why did you go to a *strip club*?"

I grin. "Final taste of the sins I'll leave behind."

Rolling her eyes, she leaves my room.

I throw my legs over the side of the bed. "It was a joke, Tamika."

I hear the crash of the videotapes as she drops them on the

sofa, then the thud of her house slippers as she trades them for outside shoes.

"Not even a giggle?" I yell. "Not a single ha ha?"

The front door slams shut, locks clicking into place. I catch up to her in the parking lot.

"Where are you going?" I yell.

She climbs into her car, reverse lights shining white. I try to block the car with my body. Tamika cuts her eye at me then drives on. Hurrying down the street, I hail a taxi and follow.

An hour later, in the cemetery, I keep my distance from Tamika and our *Mother of Three*. I watch Tamika crumple. I watch her weep. Glancing at the tombstone, I try to think of Mariela and feel —————. Her picture appears all fuzzy and broken, only blips of the scene coming through. Brown eyes. Warm hand. Peppermint wafting from her clothes. And then? I imagine strong hugs and soothing words as she combs my hair or holds my hand. I dream of us skipping down down King Street, or maybe past Devon House, shoes kissing the hot concrete as I look up at my mother, I look up and see ————— nothing, nothing, thick black nothing, concocting Mother from make-believe. I consider waiting by Tamika's car so I can ride back with her, maybe even give her a hug, but instead I leave her to the privacy of this thing she knows. Turning away, I find a bus that will take me home.

"Hi, Bryson," I murmur, sitting alone in the apartment. "You'll never believe what I saw yesterday." I pull him onto my lap. I saw a woman clawing at broken glass, blinded by Marcus piercing deep. "I'm glad you're not here," I murmur. You don't need to carry this weight.

I don't know what else to do, so I call Jayda. "Come," she says. "Okay," I respond—but first! I chop an onion, peel and dice three carrots, mince a half head of garlic, then put a piece of hock to soak. Sifting and washing two cups of rice, I dump it into a pot and leave it next to cans of kidney beans and coconut milk and three stalks of chopped-up scallion. For my sister's dinner. She'll be starving, I know from my own stomach, after all that hollowing loss.

"Lawd Jesus, gyal," Jayda says, "yuh stink like wha."

"Sorry," I mumble, slipping into her apartment.

"You hungry?" she says. She walks to the stove, which is next to a laundry tub, next to a cot folded up and pressed against the unpainted wall. The floors are bare concrete, the windows square with black grilles flaking with rust. There's a couch, a bright red couch, with a green and yellow Reggae Boyz poster draped across the cinder block above.

"You can't come to my work anymore if you're going to act like that," Jayda says as she stirs a bubbling pot. "Yuh cyaa just stan' up an' watch like eediat while man a do what him do," she says. "Jesus, gyal. Yuh new, eee?"

"I'm not *new*," I hiss, grabbing her arm. Her skin's still oily, carrying the scent of last night's sweat. She smiles then dips her gaze, eyelashes spreading like a curtsy.

"'Ello, honey," Madonna says, walking in through a door on my left.

"Hey!" I exclaim, letting Jayda go.

Madonna sits cross-legged on the couch, a nail file in her hand.

"How are you?" I ask her.

She cocks an eyebrow, giving Jayda a look. "Mi all right," she says, sliding the file along her thumbnail.

"How, um, how was your night?" I glance at my pants, noticing the puke stains around the hem.

"Fine." She looks me over. "Yuh stink bad fi true."

"How did you like the club?" Jayda says, watching me from behind the steaming pot.

"It was great! Super fun!" I run my hands through my braids. "So many people. Fun! So fun! It was okay. It was stressful. I think I'm starting to hate crowds."

Jayda puts the spoon down.

"I was born here. I should be used to it, but I really hate crowds. All dat hustle an' bustle, everyone yelling and shoving and getting in the way. But the crowds, all those people, I need them. Does that make sense? I love them. I need them. But I'm happiest when I'm alone."

Jayda's standing by me now, her hands on my neck. I lean into her, my voice muffled by her shirt.

"What else?" she says.

"I don't know." I wrap my arms around her waist. "I'm sorry about yesterday. Thank you for inviting me."

"What else?" She massages my shoulders, her slim fingers floating heavenly through my hard knots. I inhale, smelling garlic and something salty. I don't recede like low tide into the seas inside my head.

"I wish you could meet my brother," I whisper. "This is really nice." I give myself to her. "My brother was only twelve. I don't understand why my sister didn't come." Jayda rubs her hands over my braids then digs her fingers into my skin, lifting me up by the nape of my neck.

"Go shower," she says, pointing to a small room next to the couch. She lets me go and returns to the stove. My hands twitching with the urge to knead her soft skin, I turn around to do as she says.

Good boy, Madonna mouths, laughing as I walk into the bathroom and start to undress.

Water shoots from the showerhead in fits and spurts, temperature barely approaching tepid. I scrub my armpits and calves, feeling Jayda's hands on my shoulders and neck. I lather my elbows and the bottoms of my feet and scrub the crease where hips meet thighs. Jayda hasn't showered. She's filthy, nothing but oil and sweat and pulsing heat. Rinsing off the soap, I turn off the shower and walk through a door connected to a small bedroom. I glance down at my wet footprints on the bare concrete, my nipples soft and body flush with warmth. Standing by the dresser, I call for Jayda and wait.

"What are you doing?" she says, coming in and closing the door.

I look down at my naked body, still dripping from the shower. "The macarena, obviously."

"What?" Jayda says.

Laughing, I touch my head and hips, singing the words under my breath.

"Is *what* yuh a do?" Jayda says, breaking out in a grin.

I fold my arms in, putting my hand on my hips then winding my waist. "Ehhhhh macarena, ai!"

She laughs. I hop to the left.

"*Dale a tu cuerpo alegría macarena*," I sing, touching my arms and chest to the beat in my head.

Jayda laughs louder as Madonna knocks on the door and asks, *Is what a sweet yuh so?* Jayda puts her hand on the door like she might let Madonna in.

"No," I gasp.

She turns the handle.

I crouch down to hide, tucking my head between my knees and holding up my arms to cover my face. Something hard digs into my wrists. Looking up, I see the door closed and Jayda binding my wrists with her belt. She drags me to the end of her bed then loops the belt around a wrung in the metal frame. She stands back. She tells me to beg for it.

"What?"

She laughs again. She wants me to beg for it.

"Wait, what?"

Spreading my legs with her knees, she leans in close. "Give it to me," she whispers, coaxing me open as she slides deep, then deeper, thrusting again, and again, and then I do, I give it up, hot and quick.

"Next time you come to my work," she says, "you will be good." Breathing hard, I nod. She slaps my ass then flips me over. Putting on my best good girl voice, I beg her to start again.

SUNDAY

7 Days Left

TAMIKA WENT TO CHURCH BUT I'M BACK AT THE club. I'm going to be so good.

Jayda walks out onstage, the rhinestones in her bra sparkling in the gold-colored light. She drops into a split, ass bouncing in front of the club packed with people, so many people, all a dem a jus' squeeze up an' wine up, filthy and alive.

"'Xcuse," a man says, squeezing behind me. He drags his hand along the small of my back, fingers creeping beneath my shirt.

Body tensing, I turn around. He notices me and comes back. I'm terrified but I drop my gaze and smile. I make him think I like it. *Be good*, she said, so I cave in, I make my body small. He looks down at the top of my head and smirks. I take his wrist and lead him to the stage.

"Brap! Brap!" Marcus yells. "Brap! Brap!" with his forefinger and thumb pointed at the ceiling as the man slides his hands over my shoulders and down my back. The DJ switches to a heavy dancehall beat, dotted bass gravitating on the snare as I bring him to her. I bring him to Jayda twirling slow around the thick pole.

He sits down then looks at me and pats his lap. Smiling, I shake my head no and cotch on the stool next to his.

Jayda squats down in front of us, legs spread wide as I rest my hand on his thigh. *Are you a big man?* I press my shoulder into his chest. *Are you a real man?* He pulls out a roll of bills and I laugh. Jayda turns around and kneels and I can't believe that worked, so I laugh as she makes her ass dance in front of his face. Taking a bill, I slide it up Jayda's thigh and over the smooth swell of her hip, plucking the thin string of her thong and letting it snap against her skin. He leans back and hands me another bill. He tells me to do it again.

Jayda looks over her shoulder at me as I slide the bill down her back, dragging my nails along her skin and I glance at him, *Is this what you want?*, I reach the soft dip between her cheeks and I drag the bill down, down, *Like this?*, kneading her ass with my thumb, and he takes my hand then shoves the bill in her thong, impatient and rough.

In one smooth twirl Jayda turns around, sweat pooling between her breasts, and looks him over—taking in his tight shirt and young face and hands still smooth as new glass. He looks fresh to the scene, like he's enjoying his first big night. She glances at me and smirks. Wiping the sweat from her forehead, she makes as though she's about to leave. The dancehall booms down to my bones as I take my hand off his thigh and follow her lead. He pulls out four crisp bills.

Jayda grins and drops back down as I rest my hand on his chest. She takes a full shot glass from a waitress then squeezes it between her breasts. Mouth open, he leans forward as my feet turn cold and my hands start to burn, so, grinning, I shove him back in his seat then plop my ass on his lap. Jayda watches him as I lean forward and close my lips around the cool glass. Laughing, he rubs my back and throws the bills at Jayda's feet. He's enjoying it. So she grabs me by the throat, yanking the glass from my mouth, and she kisses me. *Brap! Brap!* she traces my lips with her tongue and I hear people cheer, I hear the man behind me yell, *Go deh, gyal!* as bills flutter against the back of my neck.

"Good girl," Jayda murmurs as she presses her palm against my face then shoves me away.

Laughing, he catches me. Jayda picks up each bill slowly, staying near me, as he digs his hands into my hips like he might not let me go.

"Ay, gyal," Marcus calls to me, "come drink!" He signals to a guard, who pries me off the man's lap then steers me through the crowd to the bar.

"How yuh do, sweetie?" Marcus says.

"So so." My hands shaking, I down a shot of J.B.'s then turn toward the dressing room.

Marcus looks at the man I left sitting by the stage. "Yuh naa finish?" he says to me.

I cut my eye and kiss my teeth as Marcus chuckles, waving to the guard to take me upstairs. Jayda stands up, calves glistening in tall heels. She runs her hands over her thighs then rests her fists on her waist. She's panting. It's nearly 1:00 a.m. She's been on since nine. But 1:00 a.m. means it's the end of her shift. She drops her smile, shoulders caving forward with exhaustion. I slip beyond the double doors as Jayda sways her hips once, twice, then turns to leave.

MONDAY
6 Days Left

SUNLIGHT FLITS IN AND OUT BETWEEN THE lumpy gray clouds as the frogs chirp quieter, quieter, sinking into the early morning hush. It's 6:00 a.m. I haven't slept. I'm in my sister's apartment, squirming against the stiff couch pillows in the humid darkness. The power's out. Tamika emerges from her bedroom, yawning in a loud *bwwaaahhh* with her arms stretched above her head.

"Mawnin'," I murmur, turning over the VHS tape in my lap.

"Lawd Jesus!" she screams, clutching at her nightgown.

I grin at her over the back of the couch. "'Fraid a likkle duppy?"

She kisses her teeth then crosses the living room toward the kitchen. "Where have you been?" she says.

Jayda's sweat still lingers on my tongue. Where have I been? I lick my lips then swallow.

Tamika starts toward the fridge, then stops. No power means no butter, no cheese, none of her beloved milk pouring cool from the plastic carton. Before we moved, she used to drink a cup every morning—always from a tall clear glass like in the ads we saw on American TV. "Not everyone can have this milk," she told me once while she sipped. But we could. Daddy worked down at that big factory where they brought in truck after truck of dark red dirt to separate and smolder as he stood at the top in his office, directing them which way to go. We had a double-door fridge and a deep freeze in the garage. We were special.

"How long has the power been out?" I ask Tamika.

She sighs then shrugs, looking around the kitchen for something to eat. Instead of cold milk and buttered toast, there's plain bread and guava jelly, Foska Oats and shelf-stable milk.

I hold up the tapes for her to see. "I got these out before I realized." *Ring Ding*. After being good for Jayda, I feel happy. I feel light. I want to sit with my sister while Miss Lou booms and feel happy with her too. Tamika opens the bread as I let my head flop back on the couch cushion.

"You know what I always wondered?" I press the middle finger of my left hand against the thumb of my right. "Whether Anancy is the same spider who climbed up the waterspout." I press the thumb of my left hand against the middle finger of my right—then switch, then switch, fingers scurrying up and up toward the ceiling. "Miss Lou said that Anancy—he's everyone and everything. That's what she always said, everyone and everything. So," sitting up, I look at my sister, "I always wondered, is he Itsy Bitsy too?"

Tamika laughs. She puts down the bread and joins me on the couch. "Akúa," she says, "Your Highness, aren't you too old to be filling your head with fairy tales?" She reaches for the tape, her thumb tracing the worn-out label.

"This is what she gave us," Tamika says. "Anancy and Miss Lou, these were her favorite things." She turns the VHS over in her hand. Outside, a truck horn blares, lights reflecting through the window from the street below.

Feeling through the dark, I weave my fingers through my sister's and pull her hand close. "Tell me about her."

"Hmm?"

"Mummy. Tell me."

"What do you mean *tell you?*" Tamika says. "You were there."

I bite my lip, my palm growing hot.

She sighs. "You were young, I guess. And Mummy, she was already so sick." She puts down the tape and slides a little closer. "She was . . . I don't know. She was hard. Not hard. Stern. She had high standards, and we, her children, we were to meet them. One time, in third form, I earned a ninety-seven on a calculus test. Ninety-seven! Highest score of the whole class. But when I told Mummy, she just looked at me and said, *Wha 'appen to de oda three points?* She laughed after, softening it with a joke, but I could tell she meant it. She made us sharp. She demanded excellence. So we were. I tested so well that I skipped the first grade and you could read whole books by the time you were three." Tamika smooths the baby hairs by my ear. "She was hard because she loved. Jamaica nuh easy, yuh nuh. Nuff smaddy a fight fo' de same likkle something dem. She loved us hard so that we could enter any room with courage and grace and say, *I am here.*"

Sighing, I rest my head on Tamika's shoulder. I would've liked to know this mother. She sounds mean. She sounds glorious. Down the hall, the surge protector screams to life, signaling that the power's back.

"You hungry?" Tamika says, getting up.

"Wait." I rub my empty stomach. "What else?" I murmur, watching her walk into the kitchen.

Tamika lights a match and touches it to a burner on the stove. "How yuh mean?"

"Mummy. What else?" Did she yell like Daddy? Love food like Bryson? Was she closed up like you, always wound tight and far away? Tamika puts the kettle on the stove as I walk into the kitchen. "Tell me everything."

Were there soft crevices to her love, hidden like secrets beneath her sharp tongue? My stomach grumbles. Was she wanting, like me? Did she look at the world around her and wonder, *What else?* I squeeze my sister's shoulders.

"Akúa, I . . ." Tamika drops a tea bag in her mug then holds her hands up by her chest.

I look at her empty palms, brown creases crossing pink skin, nothing there to give. Tamika takes a step back against my sudden need.

"I don't know, Akúa," she says. "She was just . . . I don't know. She was our mother. She was everything. I don't know how else to explain."

The kettle whistles. Tamika edges away from me, reaching for the knob on the stove. I feel myself swimming, beginning to slip away. Turning toward the dining table, I sit down and rest my head on the cool wood. I am hungry, I am craving. *What else?* My sister sighs then puts her hand on the back of my neck. Outside, gray clouds give way to quiet drizzle as rain falls past the window like silver webs glinting.

TUESDAY

5 Days Left

THE PORRIDGE BUBBLES AND THE TOASTER SIZ-
zles and Tamika hums happily as she twirls in her
pleated skirt. We're going to church. Outside, lightning
cracks as thunder rumbles. Coming storm; third of the season;
Tamika smiles as though basking in summer sun. We're going
to have me baptized. Serving myself porridge, I watch Tamika
as she butters her toast. Did Mummy work in a loud plant like
Daddy? Did she smack her lips while she chewed? *What else?*
The twitch of Tamika's elbows tells me she's wary, that if I push
too hard she will close up against my rumbling need. I sprinkle
brown sugar over my porridge. I forgo my usual coffee for a cup
of black Tetley. Swallowing hard, I make the questions stop.

"Let us pray," Tamika says. I stare at the crown of her head as
she says grace, lips moving in muted excitement. I will be washed
with the water of her Lord as a token, a gift. She looks up.

"Amen," I mumble as she starts to eat.

When we arrive at her church, the stage is empty and pastor

nowhere to be found. A woman moves between the pews, her brooch hanging low as she places hymnals on every third bench. I take a seat in the nearest pew as Tamika goes to a man lining up music stands onstage. He smiles then gives her shoulders a light squeeze.

"My sister," Tamika says, pointing to me but never calling me over, "she's being baptized today."

He releases a long *ahhh* then gazes at me like a doting father. "A blessed day to be washed with the glory of Christ," he exclaims.

I smile and wave, playing the part. This is a treat for her. Thunder rumbles. A couple rushes in, their clothes damp and heads covered in plastic bags to keep their curls intact. Tamika taps a woman's shoulder. "My sister," she says, pointing to me. Hearing my cue, I smile and wave.

A family comes in, their children grinning as they make designs on the carpet with their dirty shoes. I crane my neck to look beyond them, to see if I can spy Jayda when she walks in. She said she was coming, that she couldn't wait to see the show.

"My sister," Tamika says.

I prepare to wave.

"My sister Akúa—"

I look around for her, smile already plastered on my face.

"She's home," Tamika says. "She's finally home."

Tamika's behind me, on the other side of the church. I turn in time to see the soloist lean forward, her fascinator arching toward Tamika. I watch my sister talk about me, about how hard yet wonderful it's been to have me home. The soloist nods, murmuring something gentle and encouraging. Eyes soft and captured, Tamika lets herself unfurl. The soloist opens her arms like she wants to swallow my sister up, like she might take Tamika and savor her deep.

"Praise be," the soloist says, closing her arms in the warm space between them.

"Amen," my sister agrees, clapping her hands then hugging herself tight.

Lightning snaps. The lights flicker. Something wet touches my neck. I glimpse Jayda walking behind me, her hand dripping with rain. I don't linger on her. "In public," she'd said to me, "we must keep up a good face. Out there, we are just girls who are friends." Tamika eases next to me in the pew as the choir assembles onstage, organ sounding in three loud chords signaling the start of service.

"We must surrender to His salvation!" the pastor says. "We must wash ourselves in His goodness though *we are not worthy*!"

"We are not worthy!" the congregation echoes.

"We are not worthy!" he says again.

"*We are not worthy!*"

I am not worthy but rain falling down, down, sweet wetness blessing the church like her lips on my skin, streaming from the sky like parting thighs and we jump! we praise! the Lord her body crashing against mine rain lapping the shingled roof and *yes Lord!* the pastor wails and *yes Lord!* I hear her behind me as the rain comes harder as Jayda comes harder as she holds me, giving shape to my pleasure and *praise Him!* we are not worthy *praise Him!* we are not worthy of this sweetness falling wholesome like sugar on my tongue like hibiscus so heady and fragrant and I think of Jayda, I hear her wailing behind me like I heard her grunting, giving me glory and light.

The service continues. They drink their juice and eat their cubes of bread. They sing their songs and murmur their prayers— louder, faster, until I am next in the baptismal line. The pastor lifts a small boy out of the water and delivers him into the arms of his waiting parents.

"Fresh rainwata!" the pastor says, pointing to the plastic pool. "Straight from the eyes of God."

"Yes, Lawd!" the choir echoes.

The pastor reads from scripture, eyes wide with zeal. I want to believe him. For my sister's sake, I want the weight of his words to sing through my bones but all I see is a bald and babbling stranger. I start to leave the line. I'm so sorry, sister. Tamika's smile cracks but the pastor doesn't notice. He leans forward, grabbing me by the shoulders then pulling me so rough that I stumble up the stairs.

"In the name of Christ!" he bellows.

I hold out my hands. "Wait!"

"I anoint thee!" He plunges me into the pool.

Arms flailing, I can't think, can't breathe. Beneath the murky water, I think I can hear someone screaming. He pulls me up and rests me on the edge of the pool, opening his arms to the overjoyed room. It's me. I'm screaming.

"You have been filled with the grace," the pastor says.

"The grace!" the congregation echoes.

"The glory."

"The glory!"

"The sweet salvation," he points to the cross on the wall, "of our lord Jesus Christ."

I'm still screaming. The congregation claps and sways, some fainting and speaking tongues. The pastor keeps talking about my new life as my sister helps me down the stairs.

"You are saved!" Tamika says.

My screams turn into coughs. I search the crowd for her, their faces leering close. Jayda looks at me, eyes curved in mourning. *I'm so sorry*, she mouths.

"You are saved," Tamika says again, pressing her wet face into my neck.

I cough harder, trying to get it out.

"How does it feel?" Tamika says.

Coughing so hard that my lungs start to hurt, I feel it still lodged deep. My sister and the congregation, they're all swaying, voices jumbling as one. I hate them.

"You are not worthy," Tamika says, "but you are loved."

I hate them I hate them *I hate them*. I let my sister lead me back to the pew as I scratch my neck and thighs, rubbing my stomach and shins. I watch them, hands joined and joyously singing as I feel my skin crawl with a slick I cannot name.

WEDNESDAY

4 Days Left

I GO STRAIGHT TO JAYDA'S APARTMENT AND WE fuck. No talking, no buildup, just clothes off and go. She ties me up and makes me moan to bring me back, to plunge me deep in the power and glory of her hips against mine. Jayda sucks on my fingers and I was born in Jamaica, I am Anglican, with her I am here as she slaps my ass then pulls me on top. We fuck and I fuck to feel clean, to bring myself back to my own light.

Panting and spent, I lay my head on Jayda's chest as she collapses onto her back. She lifts one of my braids, twirling it around her finger as sweat runs down her thigh, crisscrossing like cobwebs. She tries to ask me about the baptism. I kiss her hard to make her stop. Pressing my thumb against her navel, I tiptoe my fingers across her stomach—middle finger then thumb, middle finger then thumb. Jayda sighs then decides to ask me about something else.

"Did you love her because she was white?" she says.

"What?"

"Did you?" she says.

Sara. *Saaaraaaa.* I swallow hard. "I loved her because of what she meant."

Jayda laughs. "So wha, her white skin nuh part a dat?"

Reaching through the dark, I grab her hair and pull. "Are you only fucking me because I'm Black?"

She pinches me in the ribs, squeezing hard until I let go. "I liked how lost you looked on the bus," Jayda says. "Simple and lost. Sometimes, simple is a comfort. Simple is a salvation."

I watch her as she exhales, eyes closed in bliss.

"Unnu finish?" Madonna says, opening the door and coming in.

Squealing, I scramble to get under the sheets.

Madonna laughs. "Yuh tink dis is first time me a see woman naked?" She unpacks wads of cash from her bra and stuffs it into a powder tin.

I look at Jayda. "How do y'all know each other?"

Jayda smiles. "She was my first boyfriend."

Madonna blows her a kiss then goes back to the living room. Door closed, I hear her unfolding her cot and getting ready for bed.

"By the way," Jayda says, "yuh need to buy lube."

Spitting in my hand, I reach down then give her a rough kiss.

Did you love her because she was white? I loved Sara because she couldn't undo me. I loved her because I am Black and she is white, hard facts like brick walls keeping me separate and safe. She could never gleam with the promise of recognition then leave me dejected and on the outside. With her, I stayed whole. I was whole and alone. Like how? Like this.

The sound of cicadas buzzing rose smooth through the humid night. Somewhere, a car horn blared—tinny, grating, waning through the fields and fields of swaying Texas wheat in a long, low hum. Sara took the beer bottle from me, brown glass glinting in the muted light. We were in the tenth grade. She took a sip then coughed.

"How can y'all drink that?" she said.

Y'all. Watch her—curve of her lips and roll of her tongue. *Ye all, yeall, y'all*, flowing as smooth and natural as the heat against my skin.

She handed me the bottle. "That's disgusting."

I swirled beer around my mouth, feeling my nostrils flare with every bitter gulp. Barrett leaned over and tapped his bottle against mine.

"Lone Star," he said, holding his bottle high like appraising something precious. "Drinking any other beer is treason."

"You're so full of shit," Sara said.

"No, I'm drunk." Barrett settled against the rear windshield of his truck. "Big difference."

The wind picked up, blowing the stench of muddy creek bed through the open tailgate. Lying next to Sara on the dirty truck bed, feel the grit collecting beneath elbows and bare toes.

"Twenties or sixties," Barrett said, nudging my head then Sara's with the toe of his boot. "Which would y'all rather?"

Y'all, yeall. Eyes open, slow exhale.

"The twenties," Sara said. "Flappers look so awesome."

"Sixties, man," Barrett said then smirked. "Sexual revolution."

Sitting up, I pressed my forearms against the grooves of the truck floor. "Wouldn't do you much good," I told him. "You still wouldn't be getting any."

Sara laughed.

"Screw you," said Barrett as he finished his beer then threw the empty bottle into the field.

Chuckling, I lay back down. Another breeze blew through, carrying the stink of manure and the swell of cicadas buzzing. I gazed up at the bright stars spread across clear sky and imagined Anancy throwing his web there, or there, catching on the edges of rubble so luminous, coating the wheat, this truck, in His gentle presence. I fell into the drowsy holiness of Sara's elbow brushing mine.

"So which would ya rather?" she asked me.

Overhead, two lights drifted through the black-blue sky; red-eye to San An. "I'm fine right where I am," I said.

Sara propped herself up. "Aw, really? The twenties could be fun."

"For y-all, maybe." I touched my throat. *Yeall, y-all,* too long *a* and dip after the *y*. Close, though.

Sara stared at my broad forehead and oily skin then laughed a nervous laugh, clean little *hah hah hahs* as she realized what I meant. "Right, yeah, 'cause—" she said, letting her voice trail off.

"What?" Barrett said, uncapping a fresh beer.

"Say it," I urged Sara.

She stared back, refusing.

"Just say it."

She blinked hard, turning away.

"I'm Black," I told her. "I'm Black, you're white, and the Pope's an asshole."

Barrett laughed, beer dribbling onto his chin.

"It's nothing dirty. It's just a fact."

Sara turned her whole back to me, hugging her knees against her chest. She was doing it, I was almost sure of it: creasing her brow with her bottom lip sucked in as she chewed and chewed.

"Sara," I murmured. She didn't move, so I pressed my finger against her shirt and drew the letters one by one—S A R A.

She turned to me. "Know that thing I told you 'bout being named 'cause of my eyes?" she said.

I nodded.

"I made it up."

"What?"

"I never knew my grandfather," she said. "I don't know what happened. None of it makes sense." She grabbed my beer and took a long swig. "My grandparents, they came here from Germany in the bottom of a ship. Grandma says she started feeling weird as soon as they got here. She thought it was the strange food or maybe her new job. She worked in a hospital cleaning up after women gave birth. Turns out she was pregnant herself. Grandpa couldn't latch on to the language like she did, so he drove trucks and worked construction but couldn't find anything steady. Then one day, Grandpa, he just," she shrugged, "left."

I scooted closer, the beer in my hand turning slick with condensation.

"My mom thinks he got sucked into the wrong group when he went looking for steady work," she said. "The only English he knew was whatever he picked up when people told him to shut up and go away. But Grandma, she thinks he went back, went home."

A sound rose up my throat, reluctant and trembling. "Why?"

"She thinks he missed the feel of fresh snow on his cheeks."

The wind picked up, causing the cicadas to buzz louder, louder, then quiet with the dying breeze.

I leaned closer to her, wheat tickling my bare toes. "Is this another one of your stories?" I murmured. "Are you lying to me now?"

She smiled. Barrett belched. A car zoomed past on the highway, its old engine rattling. She lied to me. She was a liar.

"You okay?" I asked her.

"Yep!" she said, bright-eyed and cheery.

There, right there—behind the too-broad smile and dead-set gaze: She was lying again. Wheat swaying like waves crashing, I looked at her and realized I could lie too. With her, I could say anything, *anything*, about Jamaica or being Black and she'd sit silent and let me reign. I squeezed her knee as a mosquito landed on her arm, big as a housefly. Squealing, she swatted it away.

I don't say any of this to Jayda. I know how it will make me look.

Instead I pull Jayda on top of me, burying my face in her neck and wrapping my arms around her waist. Inhaling, I smell castor oil mixed with lotion as she crushes me, her whole body keeping me here.

"Akúa," she says, pulling my arms from around her then pinning them above my head. She grabs the edge of the sheet and wraps it around my wrists, in and out in a gentle figure eight. She presses her nose against mine, her breath warming my top lip, then says my name again. She lets the sheet go as I roll us onto our sides, her body curling around mine for a long, hot sleep.

I don't go back to Tamika's apartment. Not that night, or the next night, or the next.

SATURDAY

FOR THREE DAYS I STAYED WITH JAYDA, COOK-ing and joking and lyming with her and Madonna, all of me swimming between the bare cinder block walls of her first-floor apartment. But now I've run out of clean shirts. I need fresh socks. So I'm back at Tamika's apartment, searching through my suitcase with the phone pressed against my ear. My father answers the call in a gentle "'Allo?"

"It's me, Daddy." I haven't called him in over a week.

"Where's your sister?" he says. "She left me a message yesterday."

I grab a shirt and change of pants. "She called you?"

"Yes, man," he says.

"Fi wha?"

Daddy kisses his teeth. "She seh yuh a go out by yuhself an' leave har fi fret."

I stuff a bra inside my backpack. She called him? They're talking? Squeezing the phone, I consider hanging up. I think about hiding out with Jayda to keep them calling and questions flying, knitting them closer across this silence I'll never understand. I hear a door slam shut.

"Where have you been?" Tamika yells. She's standing by the front door, just home from work. "Where have you been sleeping?"

Daddy laughs. "See har dere."

"Yuh nuh leave no numba?" she says. "No note? Mek mi haffi call yuh fadda fi mek sure yuh nuh dead?" She puts one hand on her hip and points the other at my head. "Yuh jus' leave mi fi fret while you a sleep inna de road like yuh nuh have no broughtupsy?"

I stare at her as she keeps on yelling. Why is she attacking me? I should be angry. I should be yelling too. I keep my voice calm and low. "I met a girl."

Tamika pauses as the phone goes quiet.

"She's funny." I smile. "I think you'd like her."

Daddy clears his throat as Tamika avoids my gaze.

"Akúa," Daddy says, his voice steady and cautioning, "Akúa, chile—"

"Come with me." I touch my sister's hand. "Just come. I want you two to meet."

She looks at me, lip trembling. She's nervous. She's scared. "Are you crazy?" she says, knocking the phone out of my hand. The phone hits the bed then the floor, dropping the call in a high-pitched *beeeeeep*. Tamika looks me over, takes me in from head to toe, then she shoves me. "Yuh lose yuh dyam mind?"

I square up to her, our same cheeks on equal plane. She

readies to hit me again but I stop her. My sister, dear sister, just come. I slap her first.

Socks in my fist, I punch her in the shoulder and gut. Eyes wide, she wallops me behind the ears and kicks me in the shin. Her shoulders fall, tension leaving, as her chest swells and she readies for a fight. I punch her hip in two *thud-thuds*. She backs up, dropping down to her knees as I rush forward. I elbow her in the shoulder as she twists her body then punches me across the knee, putting her whole weight behind her fist, hard knuckle crushing soft cartilage and I buckle, screaming as I fall flat on my back. Breathing hard, she pins me down by driving her elbows into my chest then leans in close.

"I will live," she hisses, and then she's gone, bedroom door slamming behind her.

I sit up slow, rubbing my knee and aching chest. I stuff clean clothes and my brother into my backpack, zipping it up as I climb to my feet. Marching down the hall, I hear Tamika pacing in her bedroom. I kick her door in one loud *thwack* to tell her I'd hurt her if I could.

Music vibrates down my legs as Jayda squats onstage, bare thighs splayed. I jog up the stairs, Appleton sign flickering overhead as my bag bounces against my back. Slipping into the dressing room, away from the crowds, I cradle my backpack close. My ears and elbow still hurt as soca blasts through the cool cinder block. There's no one else here, just Bryson and me.

I'm not going back to Tamika's. Let her wonder and call.

Unlatching my brother's box, I scrape the bottom and sides to gather what's left. This is where Jayda works, so this is a good place. This is a happy place. I want him to be here too. I sprinkle him between the cracks in the floor and splits in the baseboard. I smear him on the underside of the small counter, next to dabs of dried makeup and wads of old gum. The door swings open. Jayda walks in and I catch a glimpse of Marcus as he scoops and serves.

I give Jayda a small smile. "There's someone I want you to meet." My sister isn't coming, so I tell myself my brother would've if he could. Jayda's a funny kind of mean, which Bryson would've liked. I imagine them walking through the market, trading gentle barbs as their hands rove over pieces of cut pumpkin and ripe papaya for sale.

Jayda doesn't hear me as she fixes her hair then searches through a bag of makeup for something to touch up her lips. Stepping in front of her, I hold out his box.

"Jayda," I murmur. "My brother."

Eyes widening, she lets her mouth go slack.

"It's okay." I reach for her hand. "It's all right." Pulling her to me, I rest her hand on his box.

Her body stiffens. "You brought him here?"

I nod.

"Why?"

I shrug.

She narrows her eyes. "You're strange, you know that?"

I grin. "He thought so too."

Trembling, she pats his box in a courteous hello. Grabbing

her arm, I pull her closer, crushing her lips against mine. She puts her hand on my face and tries to push me away.

"Bomboclaat," someone exclaims.

Jayda nearly trips over a chair as we spring apart. Marcus looks at us, eyes swinging from me to Jayda to me, a cup of water in his hand. I don't know when he came in.

"But mi nuh mash up yet," I tell him, forcing a smile.

I feel it, can sense the air shift as he starts to look around me, beyond me, as if I'm no longer there. We're not onstage, bills cascading from glad hands. We are in the dressing room, in real life. "So what mi mus' call yuh?" he says. "Battywoman?" He throws the cup against the wall then leaves.

Jayda punches me. "I told you. *I told you.*"

"It'll be fine." I'll find a way to make it fine. "He knows you, and he likes me, so we're fine."

Her hand on her forehead, she starts to pace.

"Just trust me, all right?" I move to hug her. "Everything will be okay."

Sighing, she rests her hand on my cheek. "You sweet child," she says. "You poor thing. You don't know, do you? Yuh shoulda stay a foreign. You shouldn't have come back."

A flurry of women enter, swapping bikini bottoms for lingerie then refreshing their foundation. Jayda disappears behind a divider to change into her next outfit.

"Two minutes," someone yells.

Clouds of hair spray cover the room. Hiding in the middle of their bodies, I rush back into the thick of the club.

"Marcus!" I yell.

He pours vodka into a shot glass then hands it to a customer.

"Marcus!" I yell again. Look at me.

He uncaps a beer then slides it down the bar.

"Marcus, Lawd man!"

Madonna grabs my arm and glares at me. Forcing a smile, I ask her about her night.

"What did you do?" she says.

"Hmm?"

She points at Marcus. "What did you do to make him treat you like me?"

The bodyguard lumbers toward us. "Gweh!" he says, shooing us like strays.

Madonna slinks back down the stairs as I dart to the other end of the bar.

"Marcus!" I try again.

He slams a cup on the counter. "Nuh dutty up mi name," he says.

"But, bwoy, is jus' me."

"Gweh!" he yells. People by the bar glance at me and laugh.

I tap my bag to keep myself calm. This is a good place. This is a happy place. I watch Jayda as she twirls onstage. With the bodyguard distracted, I rush back into the dressing room and grab the nearest bottle I can. It's rum, old rum, crystallized sugar sticking to my lips. I head back to the crowd with the bottle in tow, swaying with the heat of all these bodies pressed close.

Hours later, Marcus swings his gaze across the thinning crowd then calls over the bodyguard. Downing the rest of the bottle, I glare at him. I shouldn't, but—

"Marcus!" I yell.

He ignores me, slapping the bodyguard on the back. I shouldn't provoke him, but why not? I'm here too. "Spare mi likkle wata, nuh?"

He marches out from behind the bar. "How many times mi haffi tell yuh—" He slaps me across the face. "Nuh dutty up mi name!" He slaps me again.

I shove him in the chest. He is not my sister, sharing one blood. I kick him in the thigh. He is not Jayda, soothing in her control. I punch him once, twice, until he's cowering. I punch and I kick and I say no. Stumbling forward, I keep swinging, too heated to stop.

"Rahtid!" someone yells. "'Ooman a beat pon Marcus like drum."

People turn and watch as Marcus gets up and spits in my face. He is thin. He is short. He bends to my rage as I knee him in the crotch. He doubles over, yelling, "Yuh stupid pussyhole gyal—" Then I lose him, patois spiraling around my ears. Someone pushes me back as people circle around him, protecting him as they laugh. I need to find Jayda. We need to leave. She's onstage, still an hour left in her shift, so I find a corner where Marcus can't see me. I flex my fingers, knuckles bright red.

A while later, the DJ switches off the music as the lights come up on the emptying dance floor. I stay where I am, hidden from sight, until Jayda climbs the stairs.

I grab her arm. "We have to go." We can hear two men talking in the stairwell that leads outside.

"Oi!" It's Marcus. "Dutty gyal, come yah so."

The bodyguard moves to grab Jayda but she clings to me, her nails digging into my arm.

"Leave har," Marcus says, leaning against the door to the alley. The bodyguard moves behind us, blocking the walkway back to the club. Marcus climbs the three stairs then takes us both by our elbows, soft and careful. "Come yah so."

Jayda hits him in the chest as another man steps between us—taller, thicker, his grin towering over our heads.

"Ay, pretty gyal," he says, grabbing me by the neck, "yuh lose yuh way?" Jayda yells something, her patois snarling as she punches him in the side. He looks down at her and laughs. "Mi hear seh yuh a lay wid 'ooman. Yuh mumma neva mek yuh study Bible inna primary school?" He lets me go as Marcus takes off his shoe.

"Marcus," Jayda pleads as I rub my bruised throat.

Standing on his tiptoes, Marcus shatters the light bulb with his shoe heel. In the darkness, we hear the quick *zzzp* of pants being undone. Jayda grabs me again, squeezing so hard I feel my shirt ripping beneath her nails. Marcus and the other man move around us, their hands on my arms, her back, my thighs, her chest, feeling us in the failing light. Marcus moves back to let this man have first taste. He doesn't beat us, doesn't hold us down, giving us room to fight as he grows excited at the chase. *Are you crazy?* my sister said. And I am crazy. I am. So this is what I do.

Grabbing the nearest thing I can, I bring my brother down on this stranger's head. The wood breaks on his skull in a satisfying squelch as Jayda starts to scream. Marcus lunges toward me as Jayda screams louder, higher, the sort of screech that stops you dead. He flinches and I jump backward, swinging and shoving as he grabs at my hair and breasts. The bodyguard comes rushing. Jayda drops down and punches him in the thigh. He trips as Jayda jumps on his back then beats on anything her hands can reach. Marcus wrangles me to the ground and tries to climb on top of me, my arm brushing against my brother scattered on the cold concrete. He yanks at my pants and *I say no* so I grab a shard of my brother's box and drive it into Marcus's arm.

"Rahtid!" the other man says.

I say no *I say no* so I pick up another piece of the box. Jayda stops screaming and grabs a piece too. The other man hurries with his pants as she stabs him, throwing her whole weight into driving the wood between his ribs. He pushes open the alley door and stumbles outside. Jayda looks around, her eyes wild, as I collapse onto the floor and Marcus wails.

I want to squash Marcus. I want to feel the sweet crunch of his body struck dead. But the door at the top of the stairs opens, more men rushing out. Jayda and I slip out into the alley. We see Madonna against a wall, her pink hair between a man's legs. She looks at us, mouth full, and gestures for us to go.

We do. We run! Our legs pounding on loose gravel, we sprint out the alley, up the road, across the street, and into the warm glow of downtown light. I reach out to grab Jayda's hand. She shoves me away.

"Go," she says, "run!" She takes the left of two roads.

I move to follow her and she stops me, chest panting. "Go

home," she says. "Run! Go!" I look down the lane on my right leading to Queen Street, then Constant Spring, then up, up, *up*! "Go home!" she says, already backing away. "Don't follow me. Just go home. Go!" Orange streetlight covers the black asphalt, filling the divide. From across the pool of light she looks at me, and waves.

One of my most vivid memories of my brother was when he was seven and I took him to a hockey game. I don't know why this memory stands out. Hockey is a dumb game. I should remember his first day of school or a big fight we had or the day my mother brought him into my life, swaddled in soft blankets and smelling of sweet milk. But it's this night, this dumb game that I remember most. I can still smell the wintry cold and feel the fat rolls on his chin. It was a Wednesday in March, my university acceptance letter freshly pinned to my bedroom door. Bryson looked at the letter, his brow furrowed as he looked at it long and hard. He knew what it meant. I slapped him on the shoulder and said, "I'm leaving in five, with or without you."

We buckled up and I don't remember the route, but I remember how far away from the arena we parked. It was the only lot where parking was free. Holding my brother by the shoulders, I guided him across the parking lot soaked with slush. He skidded, his left foot nearly flying out from under him. I held on tighter, keeping him upright as we waddled toward the arena's entrance.

We took our seats, my brother and me, two fold-down plastic chairs with a third next to the concrete aisle. Our father was supposed to be there. He'd won the tickets from a raffle at work.

But he wasn't there, because he was at work. Bryson asked him why, saying it made no sense for them to give him tickets then make it so he couldn't go. Daddy sighed, chewing his words to make them soft for his son to understand.

We stacked our jackets on Daddy's empty chair. A player moved in for a goal, chucking the puck into the small net. Was that our team? Were we supposed to cheer? Everyone around us stood up and screamed, so we cheered. Go us, whichever we were.

"This is a weird game," Bryson whispered.

Chuckling, I patted the back of his neck. "I know."

"Can we get hot dogs?" he said.

"You paying?"

He rolled his eyes as a player moved in for another goal, but missed. The crowd erupted in boos as I pulled a five out of my pocket. Bryson grabbed it and started up the stairs before I had a chance to tell him to put my onions on the side. Two players smashed into the barrier in front of me, leaving red streaks on the plastic screen. I wondered if they lost blood so often that they didn't even notice, as common to them as lacing up and heading out. Or maybe it wasn't blood at all but small packets of ketchup shoved between their teeth to put on a good show. Bryson rested my drink in my hand.

"They only had Coke," he said, "so I got you regular with no ice."

I smiled. He knew I preferred Pepsi.

"Where's my change?" I asked him, taking a sip. "And my hot dog?"

He threw me a sly smile then forced a tortilla chip into my mouth. "This looked better." He dug into the nachos on his lap.

I grabbed another chip and dunked it into the extra cheese as we watched the black puck flying around the frozen oval. We clapped when other people clapped, booed when other people booed. At the end of the first half, we stood and screamed along with everyone else as the players left the rink.

Music blasted over the loudspeakers as a group of cheerleaders took the ice, carrying mini-cannons and balled-up shirts to shoot at whichever section made the most noise. I started screaming, hoping to win a shirt for my brother. He screamed then coughed, throaty and deep—the kind of cough that would make a mother concerned.

"Cold in here, huh?" I asked him.

He nodded, so I draped my jacket over his shoulders as he crawled onto my lap. His head towering over mine, he leaned down and tried to curl up against my chest, like he used to when we were young. He knew I was going to leave him. He knew that in a few months, I was going to start at a new school, far away, without him. He pressed his forehead against mine—gentle at first, then hard, insistent, like he wanted to leave a mark, like he never wanted me to forget.

I think about that pressure, focus everything on his forehead against mine instead of the pain in my calves as I run and run. Panting hard, I look around for a watchtower or street sign so I can figure out where I am as I remember the soft crack of stale chips and salty glop of nacho cheese, bullhorn sounding to signal the start of the second half. I miss you, brother.

Legs aching, I finally slow down. I don't recognize any of the street names. Stumbling across the road, I barricade myself inside a phone booth. They might find me, Marcus might find me. There's no light in here and the glass is so scratched that I can't see outside and when I breathe through my nose, holding my heaving chest, when I make myself breathe deep, I can smell the faint stench of old pee. Pressing my hands against the walls, I try to steady myself. *Ohmygodohmygod, what have I done?* I pull out my wallet then dial the number on the back of the calling card.

"'Allo?"

"Daddy," I exclaim.

"Why yuh a call me at such a hour?" he says, his voice comforting in its sternness. "Yuh nuh know how fi read time?"

"Someone tried to rape me."

He goes quiet. "Are you safe?"

"I don't know." I look around the small booth.

"Are you hurt?"

"I got away. Oh my God, Daddy." I hold my pounding head.

"Do you see now?" he says.

"Daddy, don't," I whisper. "Please don't. I've been hurt. Yuh undastan'? Your daughter's been hurt."

"Come home," Daddy says. "Come home now. Where's yuh sista?"

"I don't know."

"How yuh mean?" he says. "Yuh not wid har? Gyal, yuh crazy?"

I am crazy. I am. So I brought my brother down on their heads. "Daddy," I mumble, "I think I'm in a lot of trouble."

"Go a yuh sista an' stay dere. Stay dere! Yuh hear me? Stay wid har till me tell yuh wha' fi do." Glancing up, I see a dark shadow move across the glass. Someone's outside the booth. I shove the door open and run.

I turn down one road, then another, not stopping till I see a familiar sign, then a familiar store, then I'm on High Street and it's starting to make sense, I can find my way. Down the alley, up the straightaway, I run then jog then walk as the sun begins to rise, warm light on a humid day.

Before I even open the apartment door, I can hear my father yelling.

"How could you let this happen?" Daddy's saying. "How could you have been so stupid?"

"Tamika?" I mumble, coming in.

She's still in her nightgown, her hair wrapped in red silk. Her body's rigid save the rise and fall of her chest. Lips pursed and eyes glazed, she's shut up in a room I can't see.

"Tamika?" I touch her hand. "I lost Bryson. I didn't mean to, but he was all I had."

"If you had just come," Daddy says, "if yuh hadn't been so dyam stubborn fi stay back in Jamaica, den yuh sista would neva run off to God knows where doing God knows what."

Tamika exhales hard.

"How yuh so selfish?" he says, "Just tink of yuhself and not yuh own bredda an' sista. Couldn't be me yuh come from. Mus' be from stick up under yuh modda arm—"

"You know," she says, cutting him off, "I'd normally tell you to give everyone my love, but there's no one left, is there?" She hangs up then turns to me, gaze still distant. "I have been instructed to return you to Norman Manley," she says, "to pack your things then put you on the first flight home."

Walking to the kitchen, I grab a bread knife and a cast-iron pan.

"Let's go find him," I tell her.

She blinks, coming back. "What?"

"Some eediat bwoy tried to hurt your sister. Let's find him!" I brandish the skillet in the air.

"Akúa."

I stab the air with the bread knife.

"Akúa," she says again, softer this time as she wrestles the knife out of my hand. My body caving, I collapse against her warmth.

"I could smell them," I murmur. "Marcus hadn't showered. He smelled of sugarcane and beer." She coaxes the skillet out of my other hand. "The other one smelled like tobacco. The cheap kind, cheaper than Craven 'A.' His hands were rough like he works with the sea."

She wraps one arm around my shoulders then leads me down the hall. Her body's still pulsing, rapt with anger, as she opens the bathroom door.

"Do you think they'll come for me?" I ask.

Mouth sealed in a hard line, she sits me down on top of the toilet. She wipes the snot from my nose then dries my eyes with my shirt. She takes off my watch and my socks, then lets my braids loose from their bun. Easing my pants down my legs, she folds them in a neat pile and takes off my shirt, my bra, then hooks her thumbs on my panties to lay me bare. She pauses, finally letting her gaze meet mine as she spreads my legs apart. Bending down, she inspects my calves, my stomach, then she peeks between my thighs to make sure I'm, that I'm not— She nods, satisfied, then puts the stopper in the tub to draw a warm bath. Pulling me up to standing, she helps me ease into the collecting water.

"Tamika—"

She puts her finger to my lips then shakes her head no. Squirting dishwashing liquid over my head and into the water, she stirs the soap till it suds in soft peaks. She cups her palms, pouring warm water down my back. With her bare hands, she cleans me. Lifting my arms, she scrubs my armpits with her nails. Moving my breasts, she cleans the crease where stomach meets chest. She reaches behind my ears and between my toes, scraping away every bit of grime until I am pure, I am glorious. Closing my eyes, I rest my head against her neck.

"Give thanks and praise," she says, "you did not die." She covers my nose and mouth then eases me down beneath the warm water. I don't scream, resting easy in her hands, as she pulls me up, clean and new.

"Hallelujah," I murmur.

She kisses my forehead, clearing soap from my eyes. I take a breath, my whole body easing forward in deep relief. Waves crashing like blood lapping, I am the sea.

ACKNOWLEDGMENTS

I am deeply indebted to the many bright souls who buoyed me—artistically, spiritually, and sometimes literally—as I endeavored toward the book you now hold in your hand.

First, thanks to my mother. Who knew that what started as a busywork tactic during those long summer months between school sessions—sitting me in the living room with stacks and stacks of books, more books than any child could ever read no matter how voracious their imagination—would become the seed of my life's vocation.

Thank you to Mrs. Dooling, my English III AP teacher who was the first to look at my writing then at me and say, "Keep going."

Thank you to the University of New Brunswick's English MA program and the Iowa Writers' Workshop for providing me with the space and structure necessary to deepen my practice. To MacDowell for the gift of time to do nothing except write. To Restless Books for selecting an early draft of this novel as a finalist for the Prize for New Immigrant Writing. And to the Writers' Trust of Canada and McClelland & Stewart Journey Prize for recognizing "Homecoming," an excerpt from this novel, as one of the best in emerging Black Canadian literature.

Thank you to Sam, Margot, Yiyun, Jen, Sue, and the many teachers and mentors over the years who spurred me on.

Thank you to the editors at *The Caribbean Writer*, *PRISM International*, *Epiphany: A Literary Journal*, and *Aster(ix)* for publishing early excerpts of this project.

Thank you to my agent Monika for keeping the faith even when I couldn't, and to my editor Alicia for being such an enthusiastic collaborator in molding this novel into the best version of itself that it could be. And of course, thank you to everyone at Catapult—Laura, Dave, Rachel, Megan, Vanessa, Kendall, the list goes on—for all your work behind the scenes in stewarding this project into the world.

Finally, my deepest and everlasting thanks to Ayana, my first and most important reader. My great love. May we never stop laughing, through rough seas and calm.

© Eli Jules

CHRISTINA COOKE's writing has previously appeared in *The Caribbean Writer, Prairie Schooner, PRISM international, Epiphany: A Literary Journal*, and elsewhere. A MacDowell Fellow, Journey Prize winner, and Glenna Luschei Prairie Schooner Award winner, she holds a Master of Arts degree from the University of New Brunswick and a Master of Fine Arts degree from the Iowa Writers' Workshop. Born in Jamaica, Christina is now a Canadian citizen who lives and writes in New York City. Visit christinajcooke.com to learn more.